THE BOSS

CARFANO CRIME FAMILY
BOOK 2

REBECCA GANNON

Copyright © 2021 Rebecca Gannon

All rights reserved.

ISBN: 9798500061928

No part of this book may be reproduced or transmitted in any means, electronic or mechanical, including photocopying, recording, or by any information storage and retrieval system without the written permission of the author, except for the use of brief quotations in a review.

This book is a work of fiction. Names, characters, places, and incidents are either products of the author's imagination or are used fictitiously. Any resemblance to actual persons, living or dead, events, or locales is entirely coincidental.

More by Rebecca Gannon

Pine Cove
Her Maine Attraction
Her Maine Reaction
Her Maine Risk
Her Maine Distraction

Carfano Crime Family
Casino King
The Boss

To everyone who's been broken by the only one who can heal them, this is for you.

THE CARFANO FAMILY

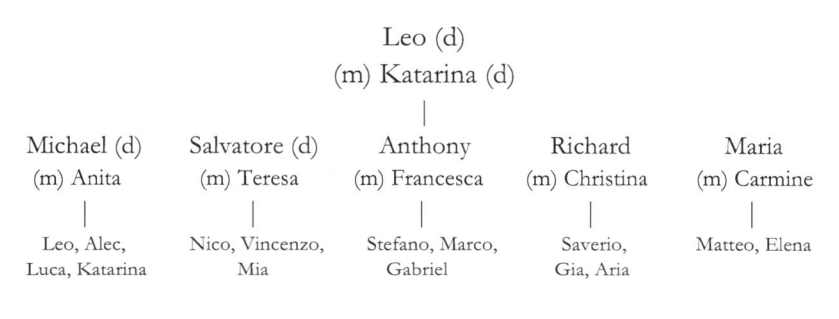

Leo (d)
(m) Katarina (d)

Michael (d)	Salvatore (d)	Anthony	Richard	Maria
(m) Anita	(m) Teresa	(m) Francesca	(m) Christina	(m) Carmine
Leo, Alec, Luca, Katarina	Nico, Vincenzo, Mia	Stefano, Marco, Gabriel	Saverio, Gia, Aria	Matteo, Elena

(m) – married / (d) – deceased

*"she's a flame
not the kind you flee from*

*her fire is the torch
that can set you free*

*her fire is the light
that will guide you
if you love her enough"*

- r.h. Sin

PROLOGUE
Abrianna
5 years earlier...

"Leo?" I call out sleepily.

Reaching out next to me, I come up with cool sheets instead of his warm body. I listen for the shower running, but all I hear is silence.

Rubbing my eyes, I climb out of bed and walk around my apartment.

He's not here, and panic starts to set in.

Leo's never left without waking me up first. This whole week, he's come to me every night closed off and angry. He wouldn't say anything to me. He'd just wake me up, strip out of his suit, pull the covers off, and then lose himself inside of me until we were both spent and passed out with our bodies tangled together.

Getting lost in each other without having to even say anything wasn't new for us, but this week he was different, and I've had a bad feeling in the pit of my stomach for days.

Sighing, I go to crawl back in bed, but a piece of white paper on the nightstand catches my eye. I stare at it for a moment before reaching for it with a shaky hand. My eyes blur with tears instantly, and I have to blink them away to read and reread the three words that are tearing my heart apart.

Times up, angel.

No.

No.

The note slips from between my fingers as I fall to my knees on the carpet next to my bed – the pain not even close to what I feel inside of my chest.

My heart twists like it's wrenching itself dry of blood, and my eyes flood with tears, spilling down my cheeks in silent rivers. I can't even make a sound as it feels like I'm being ripped apart. My throat is dry and is squeezing closed like someone's hands are wrapped around my neck.

He told me it would end. But I thought…I thought I had more time. I thought he'd changed his mind. But I was always just temporary to him.

CHAPTER 1
Abrianna
Present time...

"Thank you for coming with me!" Shelby yells excitedly.

"Like you gave me a choice," I say, rolling my eyes, but then smile when she gives me her famous shut-the-fuck-up-and-relax look.

We're in Atlantic City for her birthday, and after an afternoon at the spa and dinner out at a nice restaurant, we drank champagne and changed into the dresses we bought in the city last weekend. They're what inspired this impromptu birthday trip to begin with.

Mine is a relatively simple black dress, but it hugs every one of my curves, whereas Shelby's is covered in black sequins and hits her mid-thigh, with a slit that almost reaches her hip. It's so low-cut, it's making *me* nervous that she'll give everyone an eyeful of her girls. But Shelby isn't someone to ever care what others think about how she dresses. She has more confidence than anyone I've ever met and goes after what and who she wants, when she wants to.

As we walk down the hall of the club that's inside of the hotel we're staying at, the music and bass get louder with every step as we come to the top of a large staircase. I look down at the dance floor below where lights flash across a sea of people drinking, dancing, and letting go.

Smiling at each other, we descend the stairs, and at the bottom, Shelby takes my hand and guides me over to the bar.

"I see a lot of hot guys here, Abri! I could get us each one like that," she says, snapping her fingers.

"I'm good." I laugh, slapping a twenty down on the bar for our first round.

"You're far from good," she says, rolling her eyes as she takes a long sip from her drink. Grabbing my arm, she pulls me out onto the dance floor. We get bumped around a little, but when we make it to a relatively less dense spot, she spins around and dances with me for all of five seconds before she grabs the guy next to us and dances with him instead.

Typical Shelby. She's always on the hunt for her next conquest, always hoping it'll amount to something more. But it never does.

She was my first hire when I opened my family's foundation branch in New York City, and we clicked right away. Even Sam liked her when he first met her, and he's a hard sell.

Sam and Shelby have been there for me through

everything. They were the ones who pulled me out of the dark hole I dug myself into when Leo left me.

They never met him, and I never told them who he was, but they knew I loved him, and they were there for me without question.

I've known Sam since I was sixteen and he was the hot twenty-year-old college intern at my family's charity – The City's Angels – in Los Angeles, and I was just the high schooler helping out on the weekends.

I used to crush hard on him, but over the years it died down, and we became friends. Then after I graduated from NYU, I knew I wanted to stay in New York and open a branch of the charity in the city, and knew Sam was the only person I could trust to help me. He believes in the work we do as much as me.

We raise money and supply support for shelters, food banks and pantries, soup kitchens, veteran homes, and youth centers all across New York City. My father is the founder and CEO of the largest brokerage firm on the West Coast, and my mother started the Fleming Family Foundation to give back.

Having money and influence is great, but using that to help others is where the true reward and value in life lies. Sam feels the same way. His father is a big-time movie producer in L.A. and his mom is a former model. He watched them throw money around like it was confetti his entire life on parties and the best of the best of everything, while looking down on those who couldn't afford what they could.

His parents hated that he came to New York to work with me, but when they discovered they could use it to their benefit, they accepted it. They had an excuse to travel to the city more often to rub elbows with all the old money and elite of America. It was just another stepping stone for them.

Thinking about Sam makes me feel a rush of regret. He's made his feelings for me known, but I don't feel the same. I did when I was a teenager, and he knows that, but not anymore. Not since…*him*.

Sam was there for me even when I didn't want anyone to see me like that. He'd come over and just sit with me so I wasn't alone. We'd order food and watch TV, and then he'd leave when I fell asleep. He and Shelby took turns. I owe them everything.

They made me return to the world of the living. They're the reason I'm still here today. I can't reciprocate Sam's feelings, though, no matter how much I wish I could. It would be so much easier if I could.

But I'm not capable of that again.

I already gave every piece of my heart and soul to a man who took it eagerly, but never gave it back when he decided he was done with me.

Sucking down the rest of my drink, I let the music carry me away with the deep beat, trying to find a semblance of peace in a room full of people essentially needing the same thing I do – to forget.

When my feet start to hurt after a few songs, I signal to Shelby, and we start to make our way over to the bar again. We're stopped along the way, though, by two guys who look like they just stepped off of an Italian runway. Impeccably dressed in black button-down dress shirts and black slacks, something in me stirs at how they remind me of the very man who still haunts my dreams.

"Hey, gorgeous," the one says to me, giving me a sly

smile. "I'm Nico, and this is my brother, Vinny." He points to the man next to him.

Shelby practically eats Vinny alive with her eyes as she holds her hand out to him. "I'm Shelby, and this is my friend, Abrianna."

"Beautiful name for a beautiful woman," Nico says to me, and the way he does, reminds me of *him* again. "Would you ladies like to come up to VIP with us? It's our cousin's birthday and a lot less crowded than down here."

"It's my birthday, too. What a coincidence," Shelby purrs, taking a step closer to Vinny. "We'd love to celebrate somewhere a little more private," she answers for the both of us. "Right, Abri?"

My eyes linger on Nico's face and his smile grows.

"Sure," I say, and he flashes me a grin I'm confident has gotten him laid more times than I care to ever know about. I don't plan on being one of the many, but I can pretend for a few hours. For Shelby.

Vinny and Nico lead the way through the crowd and back up the stairs. A bodyguard I didn't notice when we first arrived nods at the men and holds a black curtain open for us. Stepping through, I see that it's a private balcony area overlooking the entire club, and I can actually breathe now without all the bodies pressed against me.

"My family may look a little intimidating, but don't worry about them. No one will bother you. Besides maybe me, of course," he says smoothly, and I smile up at him.

Nico places his hand on my lower back and I surprisingly don't flinch away as I take in the entirety of the balcony area. The lights from the dance floor flash in a rhythm that matches the beat of the song playing, and in between the beams, my eyes catch a glimpse of a face that I see every time I close my eyes at night.

An icy chill crystalizes my insides and I freeze mid-step.

Five years of repressed pain and emotion come flooding to the surface in a wave and I blink, knowing my eyes have to be playing tricks on me.

CHAPTER 2
Leo

Fuck me.

She's more beautiful than ever.

A true fucking angel with a halo of blonde hair falling in waves down her torso that's covered in a sexy little black dress, showing off her wide hips I used to hold and worship at like the alter they are. Long legs that used to be wrapped around my hips every night and hold me tight as I fucked her until she screamed her throat raw are on display and lengthened by a pair of sexy heels.

I lived for those screams.

I lived for her.

I still do, but that was before.

Before I took the reins and walked away.

Abrianna isn't supposed to be here. She should be back in the city, not in Alec's club, showing off her sexy body for every man to visualize naked in their beds. That's for me only. And I plan on strangling Nico later for touching her, even if he is my cousin.

She doesn't move, just stands there staring. It wasn't supposed to happen like this, but it seems the universe had other plans by putting her in my path tonight, and when Nico steps away from her, I stand. But the second I make a move, she snaps out of her frozen state and spins around, bolting back the way she came.

Without hesitating, I chase after her, knowing Alfie, my bodyguard, will be right behind me. I practically tear the black curtain apart on my way out of VIP, looking in both directions.

Fuck.

Abri is racing down the stairs, shoving her way into the crowd of people below.

She should know better. She could never hide from me.

Her blonde hair is a beacon shining out for me, leaving a trail of light behind her for me to follow with ease.

She weaves through the crowd, bumping all around to get through. But with the look on my face, everyone parts for me without hesitation.

I spot her grabbing a random guy to dance with in hopes I won't see her, but I could find her blindfolded in a dark room.

Anger surges through me when he puts his hands on her hips, and I yank him off of her. He starts to argue, but I pin him with a glare and he backs away. *Pussy.*

Abrianna looks up at me with a fire in her eyes I haven't seen in far too long. But when I take a step closer, she takes one back. I can see her getting ready to run again, and so I wrap my hand around her upper arm and start walking us towards the back hallway where the bathrooms are.

I turn to Alfie outside of the woman's door. "Make sure no one comes in," I order, and he nods.

I know Abrianna hates me, but I need to see her blue eyes again up close. I need to hear her melodic voice straight from her lips again. I need to feel her soft skin under my hands. I need to breathe in her sweet scent.

It's been so long, and I need to feel it again. That electric current that pulsed between us every time we were near each other. That fire that engulfed us every time we touched. That pull between us that felt like an invisible rope tying our chests together that would tighten and tug until we were together again. And flush against one another, we could breathe again.

She's everything I knew I could never have. Even when I did, I didn't. And I sure as hell could never keep her.

Pushing us through the bathroom door, I let go of her arm and she walks to the far wall, putting as much distance as she can between us.

"Get out," I demand, and the two women at the sink duck their heads and scramble to leave. I wait for the other two who were in the stalls to come out, wash their hands, and leave before I do or say anything else.

Alone with her, the room shrinks in size and the air around us thickens with years of distance and unfulfilled need.

"Hey, angel," I say smoothly, with practiced control, and her eyes dart up to mine.

"Don't call me that."

Walking towards her, she remains stock-still until I reach out to touch her, and she flinches away, pressing her back firmly to the wall.

"Don't touch me," she says fiercely. Her wide blue eyes are glossy and full of pain. "Why are you here?" she asks softer, hurt slipping through her carefully crafted mask.

"It's my sister's birthday," I tell her. "This is my family's casino. You're in my territory, angel."

"I said don't call me that."

"Why not? You used to love it if I remember correctly. Which I do."

"That was before," she says, looking away.

"Look at me," I demand, and her eyes meet mine again without hesitation.

They hold everything.

She could never hide how she was feeling from me. It was always right there in her eyes, even when her words said the opposite. Like right now, she may be telling me to leave her alone, but her eyes are begging me to pull her close.

"I have to get back to my friend. She'll wonder where I went."

Pulling out my phone, I text Vinny. "She knows where you are and that you're okay," I tell her, slipping my phone back into my pocket.

"Am I, though?"

I study her.

This close, I can see the subtle changes in her that the years have provided, including the shield she's wearing around her to keep the rest of the world away.

I made her do that.

"Yes. You are," I tell her, holding her eyes so she feels my words. "Let's go somewhere quieter." The thumping bass of the music is reverberating through me.

"I'm not going anywhere with you."

She's never said no to me before. And for some sick fucking reason, I like it.

"You are." Stepping to the side, I hold my arm out for her to go first, but she stays pressed to the wall.

"I don't know how much clearer I can be. I'm not going anywhere with you, and I don't want to hear anything you have to say."

"I think you do," I taunt, stepping up to her so she has barely an inch to breathe.

"You left me, Leo. You walked away like I was nothing. What could ever explain that away?"

"A lot of things."

She shakes her head. "You're only talking to me because you saw me with another man. But I'm not yours anymore."

"That's where you're wrong." I stroke the side of her neck with the tips of my fingers and feel her pulse jump and skin flush.

Oh, my angel is still very much mine.

"You have no idea what you did to me," she says softly.

She's wrong. I know exactly what I did to her.

"It doesn't matter anymore." She pushes on my chest, and when I don't budge, her eyes flare. "You're good at walking away. So, just leave me alone."

"I can't do that, angel."

"Stop calling me that!" she grits out, her eyes blazing even bluer.

"I can't do that either."

"What do you want from me?"

"Everything," I whisper, leaning in just a fraction more to breathe in her sweet scent. Like wildflowers and honey. I haven't been this close to heaven since that last night with her.

She has no idea how long I've waited to give her everything.

We remain like this – lips so close together but still so far apart. Like magnets fighting their elemental pull.

"Leo," she begs, her voice strained. "Please."

Abrianna's please is both a plea to give in and a plea to back away. I haven't decided which I'll give her yet.

She wasn't supposed to be here.

I was going to go back for her when things were settled, but it's taken too long, and it doesn't matter anymore. She's here in front of me now.

And being this close to her again is like adding gasoline to a fire that's always ablaze, providing the fuel it needs to rage like an angry wildfire in a drought.

"Please what, angel?"

Her breathing is coming in quick pants and her eyes are closed like she's trying with everything she has to resist me.

I know she'd give in if I kissed her. But I won't.

I've waited for this moment for far too long to give in so quickly.

I pull back, and with a little distance, she sighs in relief and blinks up at me with eyes that are full of confusion and desire.

"Why are you doing this to me again?"

"It wasn't supposed to happen like this," I tell her, reaching out again to run my fingers across her cheek. I can't help it.

"What wasn't supposed to happen like this?"

"Just come somewhere with me. I need to get out of here."

She pauses, then nods, letting me slip my hand in hers.

It feels like my world is finally righting itself after being off axis for five years. She has no idea what it took for me to leave her, and stay away.

CHAPTER 3
Abrianna

With Leo's hand in mine, my stomach twists and knots like it hasn't since the last time I was with him.

Every night that I've laid in bed since, he's always what my mind goes to.

Every time.

Even after I forced myself to bury everything to a place so deep down inside of me that I couldn't access it without spiraling down a hole again, he would still slip in, in those dark, lonely moments before sleep overtook me.

My dreams were then filled with nothing but raging seas and a small boat getting swallowed whole by the waves, breaking into pieces that were pulled apart and carried away in the currents. Even when the sun came out and the seas calmed, the pieces were still adrift, and it was too late for the small boat. The pieces could be salvaged, but it would never be the same. Never worthy of the open sea again.

Leo left me with my heart shattered and broken to the point of almost no return. It took me a long time to put myself back together. But I did. Piece by piece, I found a way.

I never fully healed, though, only taped the jagged pieces together so I wouldn't get stabbed every time I moved.

I'm not the same person he left behind all those years ago. I was young, naïve, and so in love that I gave myself entirely to a man who told me not to. I did it anyway, thinking I was different.

Leo always treated me like an angel who saved him. *His angel.* But I was so wrong. So very wrong.

As we walk through the club and back up the stairs, Leo's bodyguard clears a path for us. We bypass the curtain that leads to the VIP balcony and keep walking down the hall and out into the casino.

His hand in mine is the only thing holding me together at the moment. If he weren't, I think I would fall to the floor, too overcome with his presence.

My legs move forward simply because his are. I don't even know where we're going, but I don't bother asking. I know him. Or, at least I thought I did at one point in time. And as much as I'd like to think I'm the woman who could tell her ex to fuck-off because I'm better without him, it would be a lie, and Leo would know that.

He always knows.

Stepping into the elevator, the doors slide closed and the air swirls with the memories I have swimming in my head of what we used to do on the elevator rides up to his place in Manhattan. It was a long ride to the penthouse, and we were never good at waiting.

"I know exactly what you're thinking about, angel," he says in my ear, his warm breath sending a chill through me as I sway closer to him, unable to stop myself.

"No, you don't."

"I do. Because I'm thinking about the same thing." His low, deep voice does something to my insides – melting the bandages holding my heart together.

"I doubt that," I manage to say through my tight throat.

Leo places a single finger under my chin and tilts my head up to look at him. His dark eyes pull me in like a starless night, searching for light. Any light, to guide him. "I could remind you," he says simply, and I swallow hard.

No words will form on my tongue and I can't look away from him. He always was the most beautifully dark man I had ever met, but he's even more so now. The years have turned every plane of his face harder, his eyes harsher and more pointed, and his presence more assuming – bigger, heavier.

His thumb rubs back and forth over my chin, lulling me into a false sense of security and calm – hypnotizing me.

He doesn't say anything, and neither do I. The seconds drag on as we take each other in, our eyes roaming the other's face to recommit it to memory.

I wonder what he sees in mine.

In his, I see the strain of the lying life he lives slowly taking away every bit of the man he is and replacing it with an emptiness fueled by the weight of his name.

Leo Carfano – first born son of Michael Carfano, the head of the Carfano crime family, and the most feared man in

New York City and the tri-state area.

I see a faint scar that runs the arch of his left eyebrow that wasn't there before, and my fingers itch to reach up and feel the strip of lighter skin, but I grip the hem of my short dress to keep from doing so. He'd know right away that I was giving him an opening to slip right back inside of me.

When the doors slide open again, we both blink out of the spell, and Leo tightens his grip on my hand in his. Walking down the hall, my legs feel like they're barely touching the floor. As if this is all some dream I conjured up after drinking too much with Shelby. I'm sure I'll wake up soon and regret letting my fantasy get this far.

His bodyguard goes ahead of us into the room while we wait out in the hall. When he comes back less than a minute later, he nods the okay and Leo walks us in, his man staying planted on the spot right outside of the door.

As I look around, my eyes widen at the elaborate suite. It's probably the size of six or seven of my hotel room.

We're standing in a large living room area that has floor to ceiling windows, showing off an impressive view of Atlantic City, with the lights of other casinos and the boardwalk flashing up at us.

There's a kitchen and dining area to the left, and to the right are two doors that I'm certain lead to bedrooms.

A heat floods my veins at the thought of a bed being so close, but I quickly push it away. I can't let myself fall into his trap so easily.

"Don't worry, angel, we're just here to talk," he says, but I hear the devious note to his tone. "I couldn't take the constant bass back there. It wasn't helping my headache."

"Are you better now?" I ask without thought, looking up

at him with concern.

"Yes. With you, I'm always better."

Pulling my hand out of his with force, I walk over to the windows and look out at the black ocean below. I don't understand how he can make it seem like these past five years didn't happen.

I feel him coming up behind me and I step to the side, turning on him. "What do you want from me that you haven't already taken, Leo?"

"Everything else, angel. I want it all."

"You. Left. Me." I punctuate each word. "Our time was up and you left me without a care in the world."

"You don't know anything," he says fiercely, caging me in against the windows. "I didn't leave you without a fucking care in the world. You were half my world, angel." My heart kicks into overdrive and unwanted tears gather in my eyes at the mere thought of his words ringing true. "I had to leave you. I had to stay away."

"Why?" I breathe, that single word one that has haunted me day and night without fail. It holds everything.

"There were things going on that I couldn't protect you from. There still are. But I can't stay away anymore." He cups my face, his touch both fire and ice. I could so easily give in to the fire, but I let the ice freeze my need instead.

"You weren't supposed to be here," he continues. "The only way I've stayed away was making sure I was never near you."

"What are you talking about?" My head is spinning, trying to understand even a fraction of what he's saying.

"My father and uncle were murdered the week before I left," he admits without pause.

"You took over," I whisper, my hands curling into fists at my sides. "Why didn't you just talk to me?"

"There was a reason you never met my family, angel. I had to keep you separate. I couldn't do both. I couldn't be the man you needed and the one my family needed. I had to choose."

"And you chose your family," I say, but what I really mean is *you didn't choose me.*

"I did."

I turn my head away, but he pulls it back.

"Don't do that. Don't look away when I've been deprived of your eyes for so long."

"Of your own doing, Leo. You did this."

"Angel–"

"Please stop calling me that," I beg. "I can't take hearing you say it right now."

"I can't do that. I told you that already."

"Your word doesn't mean much to me anymore," I fire back, and his eyes light up.

Pressing his body flush against mine, I feel every inch of him, from his chest down to his knees. I feel both the cool glass on my back and legs and the heat of his body against my front.

"You said our time was up. Wait, no, you *wrote* our time was up, and then you disappeared."

"I always told you I would."

"In the beginning. But you never acted like it. You made it seem like I was different. Like what we had was real. Was more."

"It was."

"Bullshit," I sneer. "I never asked you to be two

different men, Leo. I never wanted a different version of you. I wanted all of you, but you didn't trust me enough to give me that."

His nostrils flare as he sucks in a sharp breath, pressing me harder into the glass. His thick, rigid cock is digging into my stomach, making my core throb and flood with need.

"I wasn't supposed to come for you until it was safe," he rasps. "But it'll never be safe. And I can't keep living in the same city as you and not have you in my bed every fucking night. As mine."

"Stop lying to me!" I yell in his face. I try and push him away, but he's pressed so tightly against me that I have no leverage.

"I've never lied to you," he growls, his eyes turning even darker at the offense. "I just never told you everything."

"Same thing."

"Hardly," he says with a bitter laugh, pulling back from me in the process, giving me just enough space to slip my hands between us and push him away.

Catching him off guard, I escape from his grasp and run for the door. But when I fling it open, I'm met with the imposing backside of his bodyguard.

Leo catches me around the waist and drags me back inside, slamming the door closed.

"You can't run from me, Abrianna."

"Then let me go."

"No." He shakes his head. "It wasn't supposed to happen like this."

"You can't possibly think I'd just forgive you and be waiting for you to come for me, Leo. It's been five years."

He doesn't need to know I've prepared myself for this,

The Boss

but he calls me on my lie, flashing me a smile that's all teeth, like a lion playing with his prey before going in for the kill.

"I know that's exactly the truth. You barely left your apartment for six months, only doing so to go to work. That girl down in the club tonight, Shelby, and your business partner, Sam, came to you almost every night just to sit and watch TV with you. And when you finally started to get back out into the world, you put on a mask for everyone to show them you were fine. But you still went home and laid in bed every night alone, thinking of me, and sliding your fingers through your sweet pussy wishing it were my fingers. My cock."

A strangled sob comes from me as tears start to silently fall down my cheeks and I back away from him. When the backs of my knees hit a chair, I fall into it, my legs no longer able to hold me up with how hard they're shaking.

He was watching me?

He followed me?

"How do you know that?"

"I know everything, Abrianna."

"You've had someone watching me?"

"Of course I did."

"Why?"

Leo leans down on the arm rests on either side of me, his face is only a few inches from mine. "I needed to make sure you were safe. I needed to make sure there was never another man."

Gasping, I press myself into the chair and he gives me a wry smile.

"You think I'd ever let another man touch what's mine? What's always been mine? You're lucky I know you're not interested in Sam and that he's never laid a hand on you. Otherwise, he'd be rotting in the Meadowlands right now."

"You had no right," I whisper. But at the same time, my heart squeezes and flutters knowing he never one hundred percent left me. "Why would you bother? Why stay away and make me think I was nothing to you?"

Cupping my cheek, Leo brushes his thumb across my bottom lip, that single connection sparking my body to life. "I needed you to not be linked to me while I took care of some business. I'm still working on it to make sure you'll be safe, but the truth is, you'll never be safe with me." He searches my eyes as if he's looking for the moment I'll realize and acknowledge him for the killer and crime boss that he is. But he'll be waiting a long time, because I've never cared. I've only ever wanted *him* – sins and all.

I already signed my name on the dotted line a long time ago. The moment he took me in his arms at my first foundation gala I hosted, I bound my fate and future to one of the devils of New York City.

The devil isn't all evil, though. He was once an angel, after all, and in the world today, can easily disguise himself behind an Armani suit and a sexy as sin body.

Leo took my sins and made them his own. He was both my biggest sin and my most answered prayer.

"I can't live without you anymore," he continues. "My younger brother, for fucks sake, was able to keep his woman safe through shit storm after shit storm, and I–"

"You never even tried," I finish for him. "You never asked me what I wanted. You never talked to me about what was going on. You just decided for the both of us and left."

"I did it for you."

"No, you did what you thought was best for me. That's not the same thing." I swallow the anger bubbling up. "You didn't even think about what that would do to me, Leo. You thought about yourself. Removing me from the equation was the easiest thing for you." Leo's face hardens before me, shutting off all emotion as the words flow out of me like a tap has been turned on. I can't stop them. "I'm not pretending to know the business you're talking about, but you should have given me the chance to handle it alongside you. I'm not some weak little angel who needs protecting or saving all the time."

"That's where you're wrong. The men in my world wouldn't hesitate to kidnap, kill, rape, or beat you just to get to me. You became my weakness," he grits out, as if the words were hard for him to even utter aloud. "And if I couldn't protect you like you needed to be…" He shakes his head once. "An angel can't fly when she has bullet holes and slash marks in her wings."

"She also can't fly when her wings have been clipped and every piece of her has been broken by the man she loves. Get away from me." Pushing him away, he doesn't try and stop me this time, nor does he try and stop me when I open the door to leave. His bodyguard looks over my head at Leo, and he must get some signal because he steps to the side and I walk away, every step I take feeling like I'm breaking all over again. But of my own doing this time.

CHAPTER 4
Abrianna

Gasping awake, I blink my eyes open and roll onto my back, staring at the ceiling of my hotel room.

Instead of dreaming about the Leo I used to know, I dreamt of the Leo from last night. And instead of walking away, I stayed.

We talked. And talking led to touching, which led to kissing, which led to him stripping my dress from my body. But just as he was unbuttoning his shirt, my dream morphed into the day I woke up and he was gone, and every day after that.

I was alone and didn't understand what happened.

Leo didn't answer any of my calls or texts, and he never

came back for me. I even gave in and went to his apartment, but the doorman told me I wasn't allowed up anymore and the access code to the elevator had been changed.

He cut me out of his life and left me with no way of contacting him or ever seeing him again.

That's what made me gasp awake.

It was just me, walking around an empty city, searching for a man who didn't want me to find him.

My hotel room is dark, and when I turn my head to the side, the clock says it's only four in the morning.

Shelby is staying in the room next door, but from the way she was eyeing that guy Vinny, I doubt she's alone or up for me crashing her little party because I don't want to be alone right now.

I'm so tired of being alone.

Dragging myself out of bed, I change into leggings and a t-shirt, throw on my NYU sweatshirt, and then shove my feet into a pair of sneakers. I slip my phone, some cash, and my room key into the side pocket of my leggings and head out.

I can't go back to sleep because I refuse to have that dream repeat itself, and I can't just sit in my room and wait for Shelby to wake up.

Taking the elevator down, I plan on burning some of my stress off at the gym, but when I actually reach the entrance and see all of the exercise equipment waiting to torture me, I bypass it and keep walking until I reach the main casino floor.

The sound of the slot machines, cards being delt, dice being thrown, and roulette wheels spinning, all float around me in a comfortable melody.

I'm not really a gambler, but my dad taught me how to play poker when I was a teenager. He used to have some of his business associates over for a monthly game, and while I knew I couldn't join them, I still begged my dad to teach me how to play. I was looking for a way to bond with him I guess, and it sort of became our thing.

After a while, I got the hang of it and was actually able to beat him. Then, on a weekend home from college, I was finally allowed to sit in on a game when one of the guys couldn't make it, and I cleaned them out.

I have a good poker face when I need one.

Pulling the fifty dollars I stuffed in my pocket out, I'm directed to sit at a low buy-in table with two men already playing, and take the seat between them.

They look at me with surprise, and I give them a cool glance in response.

They should know not to underestimate me just because of the way I look. And a few hands later, I prove to them just how much so, giving me a flashback of a night five years ago.

With my head on Leo's chest, I stroke his abdomen and feel his muscles contract under my touch as he runs his fingers through my hair.

"Tell me something about yourself," he murmurs, swirling his finger down my spine. "Something that would surprise me."

Smiling, I prop my chin up on his chest. "I'm a pretty good poker player."

"Seriously?" There's a gleam in his eyes that shows I really did surprise him, and he's intrigued.

"My dad taught me when I was sixteen. I wanted to be a part of the games he had with his other financial buddies, but he told me I was too young. He eventually agreed to teach me, though. I wanted to be able to take them all for their money they were always throwing around."

"And did you?"

"Yes." I smile.

"You think you could take me, angel?"

"Of course."

Smirking, Leo sits up and stands, holding his hand out for me to take. "You know I love a challenge, baby."

"Right now?"

"No better time," he says, helping me up. "Strip poker is out since we're already naked, so we'll have to think of higher stakes."

Sliding my hands up his chest and around his neck, I lift up on my toes and swipe my tongue across his bottom lip. "How about winner gets to choose how we fuck next?"

Growling, Leo grabs my ass and pulls me flush against him, kissing me hard, his tongue hot and demanding against mine.

Shaking my head, I leave my memory and focus on the cards in my hands, but my mind still goes there. To him fucking me against my bedroom wall and then carrying me into the living room so I could beat his ass in poker. And as agreed upon, I chose how and where we did it next. My choice was right there on the carpeted floor so I could feel the burn on my back with every thrust. I loved the tinge of pain with the absolute euphoria that always followed.

My eyes sweep over to the men on either side of me, and I see one's eye twitch and the other's brows crease. Wow, these guys are easy.

Almost too easy.

I catch all of their tells, and after winning the next couple of hands, I decide to cash out with my money quadrupled, in need of more of a challenge.

Standing, I feel him before he even speaks, an awareness covering my skin in a blanket of chills.

"They're no match for you, angel," Leo's smooth voice says behind me. "You knew exactly how to read them."

"Some men are easy to read," I say, looking over my shoulder at him.

"You never liked easy." His eyes hold mine captive. "Remember when you and I played–"

"I do," I interrupt, not wanting to hear his voice as he reminisces the same memory I just did.

"Couldn't sleep?" He walks beside me as I go to cash in my chips, suddenly no longer in need of a new challenge.

"No."

"Me either." Leo runs his hand down my arm and then leaves it to rest on my lower back. I can feel his touch through my sweatshirt, his heat burning me from the outside in as if I were naked and on fire.

Taking the tray of chips from my hand, he passes it to the teller. "Walk with me, Abrianna," he says close to my ear, and I close my eyes at the sound of my name rolling off his tongue. I always loved how he'd say it with a slight Italian accent.

Lifting my eyes to his, I feel them hit me square in the chest, churning my gut into a knot I haven't felt in so long.

"Was I not clear earlier?"

"You were. But I think you'll want to hear me out instead of running away."

"I didn't run," I sneer, lifting my chin. "I don't run. From anything."

"Of course not. You walked gracefully away from me."

"Don't placate me."

"I wouldn't dare," he says, leaning in close. "I like you mad too much. I like your fire. And I like it directed at me. You didn't have that before."

Pulling back to look at him, I study his face, seeing he's

serious. "We already talked, Leo."

"You're forgetting I know you. Just come with me somewhere."

"I'm not going back to your room again," I tell him, taking my money from the teller and stuffing it in the front pocket of my sweatshirt.

Nodding, Leo places his hand on my lower back and guides me around the casino, my body betraying me by relaxing into his touch with every step like it used to.

When we stop in front of a set of glass doors, I look up at him. "The pool? I think it's closed," I say, testing the door.

"Not for us." He holds up a keycard.

Right. His family owns the place.

I never knew what the Carfano name meant until Leo took me to his club in Manhattan one night before we went to dinner. He said he had to take care of a problem they were having really quickly, and that's when I saw him in his element. I saw how everyone reacted to him. It was a mix of fear, respect, and envy. No one looked him in the eye unless he gave them an order, some not even then. And after that night, I started noticing it everywhere we went.

I never met any of his family members the entire five months we were together. He didn't even want to tell me about them when I first asked. But one night, about a month into whatever we were, he came to me, and something changed.

He started telling me about the things he did, what was expected of him, and what he'd have to do in the future as the next in line.

I took it all.

I listened to him as he told me horrible things that would

push any normal or sane human being away, and I pulled him closer.

Leo would come to me and I soothed him, taking his burdens away for the night.

His suit was his armor. When he was wearing his custom Armani, then he was the mafia heir he was born to be. But when he took it off, he was just Leo, the man. No expectations and no pressure.

Then he'd wake up, put his suit back on, and he was once again the man everyone feared.

He's different now, though.

I don't know if any amount of time with me could really soothe him.

The pool area is extended off the back of the hotel in a long rectangle, and looking up, I see the full moon shining brightly through the glass ceiling. It reflects off the water, casting dancing fragments of light all around, and making the need for any lights unnecessary.

Walking over to the pool, I kick one of my sneakers off and dip my toes in the water. "It's warmer than I thought it'd be." Looking up at Leo, I find him watching me with speculative eyes.

He forgets that I used to know him too. When he's quiet, he's thinking. He's always thinking. His mind is a beautifully dark place that's calculated, detailed, devious, and can work out any problem or create chaos in a matter of seconds.

"Well? You wanted to talk," I goad, and he smirks, sitting on the chaise lounge closest to me.

I put my sneaker back on and sit across from him, our knees almost touching. That little half an inch of space between us is charged with an electric current I can't help but be pulled towards.

I need to touch him. I need him to touch me. I need to feel the fire again.

Our eyes meet and it's like the years we were apart fall away. But I can't give in to him. He was selfish, inconsiderate, and while I was buried under the anguished weight of not being good enough for him to keep me, he just watched me suffer.

Did he think this was some game?

Did he just want to be reminded of how much power he had over me?

Did he see other women?

"Why did you have me followed, Leo?" I ask, breaking the silence.

"I needed to make sure you were safe."

"And you couldn't do that yourself?"

"No," he clips, his temper flaring.

"Don't get mad at me, Leo," I fire back. "You could've done the job. You simply chose not to. I wasn't important enough for you to—"

Leaning forward in a blur, he cuts off my words when he grips the side of my neck possessively. "Don't even finish that statement," he says fiercely. "You have no idea how important you are to me."

Our legs are intertwined now, and closing my eyes, I feel the heat. I feel the intensity of how close we are. Our thighs are flush against each other, and as I lean in just a little more, my forehead rests against his, and I feel my defenses lowering.

Leo is a force my walls aren't strong enough for.

"I waited for you," I whisper.

"I know, angel."

His lips are just a fraction away. So close that I can almost feel them against mine as he speaks, but it's just the air swirling with his words. The words that hold so much more meaning than he realizes. He knew he was hurting me and he did it anyway. And kept doing it.

I try and say something, but I can't. My brain is telling me to back away, but my heart and body want me to lean in that last little bit and press my lips to his.

Leo runs his thumb back and forth across the front of my throat as he presses the pads of his fingers a little harder into the back.

He wants me to give in, but I gather every ounce of self-preservation that I have instead, and pull out of his grip.

I'm surprised he lets me. His hand falls to his thigh and we sit and stare at each other. His eyes are dark and foreboding, holding every promise to be the man he once was.

The man I've waited for for five years.

The man who ruined me for every other man.

The man who gave me everything I never knew I needed.

That man took my life and made it his.

That man dug himself so deep inside of me that he carved a hole no other could possibly fill. I may have taped the covering closed, but it's still there. Always there.

And now he's peeling back the tape and creeping back inside the home he once made for himself inside of me.

Leo's jaw ticks, and I know he's holding back. He's a master of restraint, but he never was with me before. I never wanted him to hold back.

Our eyes hold the other's captive.

It could be seconds, minutes, or hours, but as time stretches, the invisible rope that's always tied us together starts to get tighter and tighter until I can't take it anymore.

I'm pulled towards him without even realizing I'm moving, and when we're a mere few inches apart, our lips crash together, the desire and pull too strong to fight anymore.

CHAPTER 5
Leo

She gave in.

Finally.

My angel's lips on mine again feel as holy as finding an oasis in a desert.

My hand dives into her hair and I hold her head to mine. My tongue sweeps across her lips and she moans, opening for me.

Our tongues meet hot and heavy as we taste each other for the first time in too fucking long.

She's sweet and tarte, like a green apple I want to bite into over and over so her juices flow down my chin and she's stained on my lips and tongue for the rest of my life.

I need more.

Wrapping my other arm around her waist, I haul her off the chair and twist us so I can hold her steady while she straddles me.

Abrianna slides her fingers through my hair and grips the ends. Groaning, I nip her bottom lip and smooth it over with my tongue, her resound moan vibrating through me.

I've been hard since the moment I saw her again, but now my cock is raging.

Gripping her hip, she starts to rock against me, and I groan, pulling her hair. Her lips tear from mine in a gasp and cry, and when her eyes meet mine, they're glazed over in a haze of pleasure.

Fuck, I love seeing that look on her again.

Her fingers brush the lines of my jaw and she cups my cheeks, rubbing her palms against the stubble of my beard. Her caress brings me a soothing comfort I need more than she can imagine.

Abrianna was the balm to my damaged and fucked up soul. She saved me every night we were together. My angel swooping in in the night, her light and beauty the heavenly torch that shines into my dark and depraved heart.

I'm fucked up.

I'm my father's son.

He was harder on me than my brothers because I was the one taking his place.

Not them. Me.

I trained harder and was given the tougher jobs so I could prove to him I was worthy.

I've done things that have damned me to hell ten times over. But Abrianna's my saving grace. I know heaven isn't ever going to want me, but if an angel can accept and love me, then I'll take my heaven on earth with her until I spend eternity in the fires of the hell I created for myself.

I just don't want to drag her down with me.

Blinking, some of her cloudiness clears, and I see she's going to come out of her sexual haze any second, so I lean forward, kissing my way up her neck and over to her ear.

"You fit so perfectly," I rasp, licking the shell of her ear.

Her low moan fills my ears and I bite down, her hips rolling against mine in response.

"Leo," she moans, my name a plea on her lips. And as if uttering my name was a bucket of cold water, she stiffens, her body freezing on top of mine.

"I can't," she whispers in my ear, her cheek still pressed to mine. "I can't do this knowing you'll just walk away again. I won't survive."

I slide both of my hands to her hips and squeeze. "You can survive anything, angel."

"Not losing you again."

Her words are a knife to my gut and I squeeze her hips harder. "You never lost me," I say roughly. "But I'd fucking die if anything happened to you because of me."

"Then don't let anything happen to me. You're Leo Carfano, you can do anything and make anything happen."

Fuck me, that was the sexiest fucking thing she's ever said. Pulling her lips back to mine, I kiss her hard, giving her no room to doubt that I'm every bit the man she sees me as.

But then I feel her stiffen again, and she pulls back.

"Wait." She shakes her head. "What am I doing?"

"Nothing wrong, baby."

"I shouldn't. I can't."

The Boss

"Those are two different things, angel."

She blinks, and her eyes clear to their summer sky blue again, no longer impeded by her haze of lust.

Shaking her head, she scurries off of me and runs her hands through her long golden locks.

"I have to go," she mutters, turning on her heel.

Watching Abrianna run from me again, I let her go.

For the second time tonight.

CHAPTER 6
Abrianna

I didn't sleep a wink after I returned from the pool. I don't know what I'm supposed to think about Leo anymore. Kissing him wasn't supposed to happen, but I couldn't help myself.

There was no resisting him.

But when I let my mind clear of lust and five years of missing him, the only thing on my mind was running. I needed a little distance to think straight. I can't do that when he's near me. Especially when he's touching me.

The only thing I've wanted for years was for him to come back for me, and perhaps that's exactly *why* I ran.

I don't know what's going on, but I do know that I can't

hide in my room forever. So, after dressing in jeans and a light sweater, I knock on Shelby's door, stifling a laugh when she opens it.

"You look like hell."

"I feel like hell," she rasps, rubbing her eyes and walking back towards the bed.

"Did you have a guest over last night?" I ask, and her answering smile tells me everything I need to know.

"More like I was a guest in his room and then stumbled down here at some point in the middle of the night. You would've heard me if I were in the room next door." She winks, and I cover my eyes, shaking my head.

"I don't need the details."

"Those are a little hazy anyway. I just need to explain my sore throat somehow."

"Jesus," I breathe.

I remember those mornings…

"Enough about me. Where did you go after you bolted from VIP? Vinny told me the guy who chased after you was his cousin and that you would be fine, so I hope he was right."

That was his cousin? No wonder he and Nico reminded me of Leo so much.

"I was with his cousin, yeah. But fine…I don't know about that yet."

"What do you mean?"

I shake my head. "Nothing."

"No, don't *nothing* me, Abri. You keep everything to yourself all the time, and I want to be here for you like you are for me when I want to talk things through," she says fiercely, and I smile. "I just need a shower first. And coffee."

"I already ordered room service before I came over."

"You're a gem," she sighs, shuffling into the bathroom.

A few minutes later, a knock at the door signals the arrival of breakfast, and I set it all up on the kitchenette's counter, pouring myself a cup of coffee while I wait for Shelby.

Steam billows from the bathroom when she steps out, and she looks more human than when she walked in.

After throwing on yoga pants and a flowy white t-shirt, she settles up on the stool next to me and pours herself a cup of coffee from the carafe.

"I'm glad we have a late checkout. I wouldn't have been able to drive back to the city without this," she says, closing her eyes and sighing as she drinks her coffee black, letting the caffeine wake her up.

"There's bacon, eggs, and toast as well," I tell her, pushing one of the plates in front of her.

"Bless you." She smiles, digging in. But after only a few bites, she swallows and eyes me. "So," she starts, "I've known you for years, and the only man to ever be in your life seriously, you kept a secret and then had you practically catatonic for six months when it ended."

My eyes dart over to hers and then back to my plate of food that no longer interests me.

"It was him," I confess.

"What?" she baulks. "Are you okay? What happened?"

"We talked. He tried to defend himself for what he did to me…"

"And?" she prompts, sensing there's more.

"I ran back to my room. But then I woke up and couldn't go back to sleep, so I went down to do some gambling."

"You gamble?"

"Not really." I shrug. "I just needed a distraction. But then he was there again and we went somewhere to talk some more…"

"And?"

"And we kissed," I say in a rush, just a little ashamed to admit it out loud.

"What?" she chokes out, slamming her coffee cup down on the counter. "You kissed him? What the hell did he say to you that made you want to kiss him? I thought you hated him. I thought he broke your heart?" She asks that last one in a gentler tone.

"He did. But I…I…and he…"

"It's okay." She smiles sadly. "I understand. Trust me, I've been there. Every girl has her weakness, and he's yours."

"He has this power over me that I can't resist."

"Do you want to talk about it?"

"Not really. I'm still sorting it all out in my head right now."

"Alright. But I'm here if you want to."

"Thanks, Shel. That means a lot to me. Truly. You and Sam are really all I have, and I sure as hell can't talk to Sam about this."

Her brows crease. "Why not?" Then she gasps. "Oh my god! Did he finally tell you he's in love with you?"

"You knew?"

She rolls her eyes. "Of course I knew. Everyone knows. You were only clueless because you walk around with an invisible shield around you that says, 'not available.'"

"I do?"

"Yes. I felt bad for Sam because he's been pining for you for years. I think it started when he saw how happy you were with your mystery man, and then he was able to coax you back to life after he left. He thought that was his chance to show you he can be who you need. But you never showed any interest. In anyone, really."

"He's always just been Sam to me. I had a major crush on him when I was a teenager, but then I went to college." I shrug. "We're business partners and close friends. That's all."

"That's why I feel bad for him," she sighs. "I wasn't going to say anything until I found out who the guy from last night was, but I saw him before he ran after you…" She smiles. "He's hot as fuck."

Biting back a smile, I look away. "Yeah, he is. And the years have only made him more so."

"I spent a few hours in VIP with Vinny before going to his room"– she smirks –"and him and his family seemed…"

"A little scary?"

"Yeah. But you know I love the bad boys." She winks.

"I never met his family."

"Why?"

"They're really important to him," I tell her vaguely. "I think if he brought me around them then it would have meant what we had was going to last, and he told me from the beginning that it wouldn't."

"He did?"

"I thought otherwise of course. It never seemed like it was going to end. Which is why my destruction afterwards was my fault."

"Abri, no. Men say stupid shit like that all the time to cover their asses in the beginning. Then they treat you like you matter but are surprised when you assume they changed their mind and want more. But at least now maybe you can get some closure?" Shelby looks hopeful, but I'm anything but. "Yeah, I thought so. Just be careful."

"I will," I tell her, the lie rolling off my tongue like it was waiting to be uttered.

There's no *careful* with Leo. It's all or nothing with him, and it seems my heart doesn't care that it might get damaged even more.

CHAPTER 7
Leo

I was going to head back to the city this morning, but knowing Abrianna is still here, I can't.

She's always been beautiful, but now she's fucking breathtaking.

Literally.

I stopped breathing the moment those blue eyes met mine again.

A knock at the door alerts me to Luca's arrival, and opening it, he bursts through with a grin so wide, I want to punch him.

"So, who was that fine woman you ran after last night?"

"No one," I lie.

I never told anyone about Abrianna. Luca was with me the night I met her, at her first fundraiser in the city, but he was too preoccupied with the woman at the table next to us to notice her.

"Really? Because I think it was the woman who you've been pining for like a little bitch for over five years? Six years? Seven years? Who knows anymore, it's been so long."

"What the fuck are you talking about?"

"I'm talking about you and how you used to disappear to be with her and thought we didn't know you had someone. Then you took over for father and you didn't disappear anymore."

"Luca," I warn, sitting down at the dining table with a fresh cup of coffee.

"You should've kept her around. Then maybe you wouldn't be such a–"

"Luca," I say harshly, shutting him up. If he doesn't stop talking, I'm going to throw my cup of coffee at him.

Our father drilled into us that women were our weakness. Carfano men never let pussy interfere with business. And the moment it did, then she had to go. That alone told me he never truly loved our mother. They were more of a business transaction between our family and the Melccionas. She got to marry into the most powerful family and we got their prime dock properties.

My father also drilled into us that we have to maintain control in every situation to ensure the outcome is in our favor.

We have to be one step ahead of everyone. Always.

Sipping my coffee, I stare at Luca over the rim of my mug, contemplating my next move. I know he deserves to know. Any risks I take, he also takes. It's his job as my underboss. And Abri is a risk I'm willing to take.

I wasn't before, but I am now. All because of Alec.

That fucking bastard was more of a man than I was when it counted. He was there for his woman. He was there for Tessa when she needed him. Even when she didn't want him there, he was.

Now I need to be there for Abrianna. For both my own selfish reasons and for her.

She may fight it, and she may not want to want me as much as she does, but it's all right there in her eyes. They always give her away.

"Abrianna Fleming," I start, blurting out her name as the image of her in a gold dress fills my mind. "We met at one of those fundraisers father always had us going to."

"The only upside to those dull fucking events were the sexy as fuck women looking for a rich man to bag. So eager to please." He smirks.

That *was* the only good thing about those events. Until hers.

"She's from L.A., but came to New York for college and then opened an East Coast branch of her family's charity – The City's Angels – after she graduated. She's everything I'm not."

Luca studies me, a little too closely for my liking.

I never let anyone see how I'm feeling. I keep my emotions under lock and key, but for a moment, I let him see me.

"So, what happened?"

"She deserved a chance at life."

"What the fuck does that mean?"

"Excuse me?"

"We're Carfanos. We don't give chances. We take what we want and protect what's ours. You just walked away like some pussy?"

"Excuse me?" I grit out, my jaw clenched.

"You felt something for her and then left because you had to step up and take over for father and didn't think you could give her some bullshit fake white picket fence life that you don't even know if she wants? Does she even know who you are? Who we are?"

I grind my teeth together. "Yes."

"So you told her everything and she didn't run screaming. And yet you still decided everything for her?"

"Yes," I hiss, hating that he's hitting every nail right on the head. "We're done discussing this."

"Leo–"

"No," I cut him off, my voice letting him know this isn't up for discussion. "We're not talking about her anymore." Drinking my coffee, I try and reign in my temper.

"Fine. I'm heading back to Manhattan. I'll check in with the captains when I get there."

"Good," I clip, watching him leave.

There's no way I'm leaving here until I know Abri is too.

CHAPTER 8
Abrianna

There's a knock at the door, so I finish folding the dress I wore last night and place it in my suitcase before answering it.

I look through the peephole and take a step back. I should've known he wouldn't let me leave without coming to me again.

Taking a deep breath, I go to run my fingers through my hair, but realize I have it up in a bun, so I touch the knot instead to make sure it's in place.

With my hand on the handle, I wait a few seconds, then open the door. Why does he always have to look so good? "What do you want?" I ask dejectedly, tired of trying to push him away. I'm just so tired.

"I want you to come back to the city with me."

"I can't. I came with Shelby, and I'm leaving with her."

He holds my gaze, and his jaw ticks like he's holding back from saying something.

"I'm not letting her drive back alone just because you don't like that I ran from you."

He smirks. "That doesn't bother me, angel. I'll always chase after you. Anywhere you go, I'll be able to find you. You should have run from me a long time ago, but you never did."

The air leaves my lungs and I lean against the door frame. "I probably should've, but I never wanted to." Even after he told me who he is, it didn't cross my mind that I should run.

"I know."

Sighing, I cross my arms. He knows everything.

"I have to checkout in twenty minutes and I'm still packing."

"Can I come in?"

I know I shouldn't let him, but I also know he's not going to just leave. Nodding, I step back and hold the door open for him. I go back to packing and Leo sits in the chair near the window watching me as I gather my things. I tend to be all over the place whenever I travel.

"Have dinner with me," he says after a few minutes of strained silence.

I drop the leggings I was folding and look up at him. "Have dinner with you?"

"Yes."

I hold his gaze and watch as his eyes slowly start to thaw

from black ice to liquid black pools.

My brain contemplates the answer my heart already knows. "Alright," I whisper, and go back to packing.

When I'm done, I have nothing else to occupy myself with while Leo continues to sit and stare at me.

He always did that. He used to watch me do everything. No matter how menial the task. I could be opening my mail and he would watch me like I was deciphering some secret code that would save the world.

I always loved that. He gave me his full attention. He didn't just come to me for a quick fuck and then leave me so I'd wake up alone.

"Abri, let's go!" Shelby yells, pounding on the door.

"I have to go," I tell Leo.

"I'll call you later to make sure you got home safe."

"You don't have to—" the words die on my tongue when he gives me a look that says he's going to do it anyway so there's no need to argue. "Alright."

Standing, Leo walks towards me. Those few steps separating us are filled with the deafening air of power that seems to ripple around him with every move he makes.

He reaches out and runs the backs of his fingers down my cheek. I close my eyes at his touch. Leaning his forehead against mine, Leo cups the side of my neck and tilts my head back.

The air between our mouths is charged, and when he finally presses his lips to mine, I don't turn away, I don't pull back, and I don't run. I let him kiss me in a way he never has before. Almost gently. As if he's trying to ask me for forgiveness in a single kiss.

"I have to go," I whisper when he pulls back, stepping

out of his reach.

Grabbing the handle of my suitcase, I take a deep breath and walk to the door. He stands there with his hands in his pockets, watching me with eyes that tell me this is far from over.

I don't want it to be.

I never did.

And despite my best efforts at moving on over the years, I waited for him to come back for me.

But now it seems I have a new habit of walking away from him while he asks me to stay.

CHAPTER 9
Abrianna

Walking into work on Monday, I smile at Shelby as I pass her desk and head straight for Sam's office.

"Hey, Sam."

"Hey, Abri." He grins, looking up at me from his computer screen. He really is handsome. And I love him for moving across the country to head up this branch with me and always being there for me, but I don't love him as anything more than a friend. I just wish he wouldn't look at me like he is now. "How was your trip? Did you and Shelby have fun?"

"Yeah, you know Shelby. She had her man of the night picked out before we even got our second drink."

Laughing, he leans back in his chair and runs his hand through his hair that's in desperate need of a cut.

"And you?" he prompts.

I look away. Sam saw me at my lowest, and if I tell him about Leo, he'd probably be disappointed in me.

I don't want to upset him, and I don't want him to see me as weak. I'm lucky he still wanted to be friends after I told him I didn't feel the same about him.

"It's okay, Abri," he says gently, and I look up to see his warm brown eyes reassuring me.

"Thanks. I'm sure Shelby is probably going to tell you if I don't, so…"

"What happened?"

"I ran into my ex." That term for Leo seems so arbitrary and miniscule, but it's the simplest one I dare to use with Sam regarding him.

His face shuts down and a look of anger, regret, and sadness flashes through his eyes. "What did he have to say?"

"A lot."

"Abri…"

"I know," I say quickly.

"Whatever he had to say to you doesn't make up for what he did and how he left you. I remember everything. I was there for you. He wasn't."

I feel the crushing weight of his disapproval. "I know, Sam. And I don't know what I would've done without you."

"You would've been fine. You're strong. I'm the one who just kept showing up to hang with you."

I give him a small smile. "Thanks."

"Just promise me you won't get back with him. I know you loved him, but he destroyed you once. What's to stop him from doing the same, and worse this time?"

"I know." I look away, guilt eating at my stomach.

"But you're considering it," he says, reading my expression.

"I don't know." I don't want to lie to him.

"Just be careful." His tone sounds angry, and when I look back up at him, his face is blank.

I clear my throat, not wanting to talk about this with him anymore. "I came in here to talk about the new warehouse," I tell him, changing the subject.

"Of course," he clips. "Things are well under way with the new place. Everything from the old warehouse was transferred over last week, and we have deliveries coming in from our suppliers this week."

"Perfect. I can't wait to see it when it's all filled and everything has its place."

"Right, well, I wouldn't go over there until it's all done. It'll be a mess and I want you to get the full effect."

"I'm glad you suggested it, Sam. And you found that perfect location." I shake my head. "I can't believe how lucky we got."

"I know. It just sort of fell into my lap." Straightening the stack of papers on his desk, he avoids looking at me.

"Well, I'm glad it did. And all the funding from the golf outing event came through alright? I don't want any hiccups while we get everything up and running."

"No. No problems. We're all good."

"Good. Well, I have to go over the details of the gala." I stand. "I'm nervous to check my email. You know how vendors are just so nice to me," I say sarcastically, and he smiles, shaking off the weird vibes he was just giving me.

"Good luck," he says, and I head over to my office.

I'm so excited for our foundation's new warehouse. It's twice the size as our old one. The City's Angels helps so many places across all of New York City, and with the extra square footage, we're going to be able to hold so much more inventory and be able to help so many more people.

We have a long list of patron donors, but we also have fundraising events to get the word out. Last month was our annual golf outing at a country club in New Jersey, and in a few weeks, we're holding our annual gala. I've been going back and forth with vendors for months over prices and availabilities of the wine, liquor, vegetables, and flowers I want. Not to mention the damn band mixed up their schedule dates, so now I have to spend the next few days trying to beg and plead with whoever is decent and available.

It's always something up until the day of the event. But during it, things always seem to just come together perfectly and go smoothly. I'm praying that happens again this time.

* * * *

After a day of answering calls and emails, I'm starving and exhausted. I just want to go home and open a bottle of wine and order a pizza. But a text from Leo changes that.

Leo: I'm picking you up at 7.

My stomach knots at the thought of seeing him again tonight, but I contemplate my reply for a minute before answering. I only just agreed to go to dinner with him yesterday before leaving Atlantic City. He called me last night like he told me he would, and hearing his smooth voice crackle through the phone, I had to bite the inside of my cheek to keep from moaning. Then he'd really know how much power he has over me.

Me: I'll be ready.
Leo: I know.

God, he's arrogant.

When I get back to my apartment, I take a quick shower to relax and then put on a dress that I know will drive him crazy. I may not be able to resist him like I probably should, but that doesn't mean I have to make it easy on him. I have to torture him the only way I know will work. He can't think he can walk back into my life like the past five years never happened.

The girl I was back then died the moment he left, replaced by a woman who will never be whole again. No matter what he says or does, a piece of me will always be broken, bruised, and scarred.

It's like I'm standing on the edge of a very sharp blade, and any misstep will slice me deep. I think it's inevitable, but at this point, all I can do is pray Leo will find a way to save me before I bleed out.

He'll have to find a way to prove to me he won't ever leave me like that again. He has to earn my trust back. His words are just that, words.

Taking my hair out of the low bun I've had it in all day, it falls in a long wave down my back and I shake it out, finding I don't even have to put a curling iron to it. I apply my makeup next, playing up my eyes with a gold shadow and navy eyeliner. I learned that trick in college. It's a touch softer than black, and it makes my eyes seem bluer.

Smoothing my hands down my sides to make sure my dress is in place, an idea pops into my head. I know another way I can torture him.

Lifting my dress, I hook my thumbs into the lace straps of my thong and shimmy out of them. This dress is long enough so I know I won't have any mishaps while out, and it'll give me the extra leverage I know I'll need. Although I think it'll be equally torturous on me since whenever I'm around him, I flood with heat.

I swipe a nude-colored lipstick across my lips and stare at myself in my full-length mirror.

My chest tightens as I study my reflection.

I look like me.

The me I used to see when I looked in the mirror – confident, beautiful, smart, and capable of conquering the world.

The me I was before it didn't matter anymore.

From the moment I met Leo, he changed me. He built me up to a woman who believed she really was the most beautiful woman to him. He always said there was a light in me that burned just for him.

It led him out of the darkness he choked himself in every other second of the day. But not with me.

He would give me his darkness and I would give him my light.

But he snuffed that light out.

I see it in my eyes again right now. Whatever pride I have left doesn't want me to admit that Leo gave me the spark I needed to ignite it back to life. But pride has no place in love.

CHAPTER 10
Leo

Straightening my tie, I shrug on my suit jacket and adjust my cufflinks.

I called Abrianna last night to make sure she got home alright, even though I already had confirmation on that from one of my men I have following her. And hearing her soft, breathy voice on the line had my chest constricting and my cock rock fucking solid.

I've denied myself her sweet pussy that has the power to bring a man like me to his knees and worship her like the heavenly creature she is. I could have had her naked and beneath me if I pushed her just a little. I saw it there in her eyes. But I've waited too long to have her again to just go and fuck her senseless without her in it one hundred percent.

My hand won't do, and no other woman will anymore, no matter how close they resemble my angel. It's never the same.

I need Abrianna.

I need days to savor her, reclaim her, and remind her who owns her and always will.

When Alfie pulls up outside of Abri's building, he waits for me at the curb while I go up and get her. The doorman behind the desk looks up when he sees me and nods his greeting as I pass.

Taking the elevator up to her floor, I pass a man in her hall and all it takes is one look at me for him to shrink away and hurry past.

Reaching her door, I knock, and it only takes a few seconds for her to open it.

Fuck me.

"Angel, you're a fucking dream," I praise.

Her burgundy dress is hugging her body like a glove, and while the hem reaches her knees, there's a gold zipper that goes from her left knee up to her hip. It's unzipped halfway up her thigh, giving me a peek of her smooth skin I wish my hands were reacquainting themselves with right now.

"You look good," she says softly, like she was afraid to admit that out loud.

She's fucking eating me alive with her eyes, and while I would normally just throw her over my shoulder and carry her to bed to spend the whole night reminding her how fucking good I look while buried deep inside of her, that'll have to wait until after dinner.

Snaking my arm around her waist, Abrianna softens at

my touch and I lean down to plant a kiss below her ear.

"Thank you, baby. But you need to stop looking at me like that if you want to make it to dinner before I slide that zipper the rest of the way up your thigh and dip my fingers into your panties to see how much you like the way I look."

A strangled gasp and moan leaves her throat, and I growl, tightening my arm around her.

Anger surges through me that I can't just push her inside her apartment and fuck her up against the wall like before. "Let's go, Alfie's waiting."

I reach for the door behind her and close it, making sure it's locked, and then guide her downstairs. "How did you get up to my room?" she asks when we reach the lobby. "Hal just let you come up without calling me?"

She's referring to the doorman who's known me for years. So, no, he didn't need to check with her first if I could go up.

But she doesn't know that.

"I can be very persuasive," I tell her instead, and I feel her look up at me briefly.

"I know," she mumbles, and when we reach the car, I press her back against the closed door, lifting her chin with a single finger.

"Want me to remind you just how much?"

She immediately softens under my touch, but still lets out a breathy, "No."

Stepping back, I let her off the hook for now and I open the car door, sliding in after her.

When we arrive at the restaurant, I watch Abrianna's face when she steps out and sees where we are.

Her smile makes me want to give her everything in the

fucking world so long as I get to see that look on her face every day of my life.

"I love this restaurant."

I place my hand on her lower back. "I know." I thought if she had her favorite Chicken Milanese and lava cake, she would be more inclined to let me take her out again. And again. And again. Until she's right back where she belongs – with me. "And you know I love watching you eat their lava cake," I add.

She doesn't just eat the cake, she fucking savors it, licking her spoon clean and moaning every other bite. Last time we were here, I almost kicked everyone out so I could lay her out on the table and lick her pussy like she did the fork, making her moan for me instead.

Biting her lip, she looks away, but I brush my fingers over her cheek to feel the heat that blooms beneath.

"Let's just go inside," she says with a small smile, and my heart, the part of me I gave up on until the night I met her, starts beating stronger and faster.

Abrianna is the only person who has ever made that happen.

All through dinner, I had to deal with a raging hard-on, listening to Abrianna moan and sigh as she ate. I love a woman who loves her food, and my angel appreciates every bite that passes through her sexy lips.

After paying the bill, I stand and hold my hand out for her to take, and she licks her bottom lip when she sees my dick straining against my zipper.

I lean down to whisper in her ear, "Angel, you need to

stand up and walk out of here with me. Right now."

Her breath catches and she does as I say without any argument.

"Leo, I–" she starts, but I interrupt, leaning in close.

"I've waited five years to have you again, and I'll wait however long it takes for you to trust me with every part of you again. Just walk."

"What do you mean you've waited five years to have me again?" she asks, spinning in front of me and stopping us out on the sidewalk.

"I was always coming back for you, angel. I just needed to get a handle on things first."

Anger flares to life in her beautiful blue eyes. "And you do now? So, because it's convenient for you to have me again, you're ready to wine and dine me and manipulate me until I give in to you?"

"No," I grit out, my own anger simmering. "Get in the car. We're not discussing this out on the street." My mind is filled with images of someone gunning us down any second now like my father, and I wouldn't be able to protect her.

"Leo, stop," she protests while I push her towards the car.

Once we're inside, I tell Alfie to drive to my building and then press the button for the partition to raise. Shrouded in privacy, I rub my jaw and contemplate how to handle this.

"There are things you don't know that made me leave, Abri. I needed you to believe we were done in order for everything to work and for me to focus on my family. I couldn't risk you too. You're too fucking important. The only option other than me leaving was locking you away in a room where only I had a key." Abri slides her hand up my arm and

I reach for her automatically, pulling her onto my lap. I feel her anger dissolve as I rub circles on her back. "Believe me when I say I really did contemplate locking you away, but you deserve more than this life I live. Even knowing that, I'm never giving you up, angel." She presses her forehead to mine. "I need you too fucking much. You're the only good thing I have left to keep me from completely becoming my father," I confess, and she silences me with her lips, kissing me hard.

"I don't want you to give me up," she says fiercely, maneuvering herself so she's straddling me. I feel her hot center against my cock and I groan, gripping her hips to keep her right fucking there.

I glide my hands up her back and she arches into my touch, crushing her tits to my chest.

She starts to roll her hips against mine and I fucking lose it.

Fisting the ends of her hair, I twist it around my hand and pull her head back, dragging my mouth across her jaw to her ear.

"Angel," I rasp, "I won't be able to stop myself if you keep rubbing that sweet pussy of yours against me."

"Who said I want you to stop?" she challenges, breathless, her eyes blazing a brilliant blue in the dim lighting of the car.

Growling, I slide the zipper of her dress all the way up to her hip and palm her thigh, my fingers gripping her inner thigh, so close to where they belong.

She doesn't try and stop me.

Her eyes hold mine in a wild gaze that would make any man who isn't me think she were losing her mind. But that's just us. She's my kind of wild.

Sliding my palm up the front of her thigh, I reach her hip, only to find it bare. My nostrils flare at the knowledge that I spent all of dinner sitting across from an angel moaning into her food while her perfect little pussy was bare and wet and waiting for me.

"This dress would've shown the lines," she confesses. "I didn't have a choice."

"I don't think so, angel," I say darkly.

I keep my eyes on hers as I glide my thick middle finger through her folds. She's fucking dripping for me.

I flash her a victorious grin. "You're still my dirty little angel," I taunt, swirling my finger around her entrance, but not going inside just yet.

Her lips separate as her breath catches, and she bites her lip, trying to keep herself from making a sound.

"I want to hear you," I demand, pulling on her hair. Gasping, she releases her lip and then moans when I let my finger dip into her, only an inch, before I take it away.

Abri's cry of protest makes my cock twitch and I pull on her hair again.

"Louder." This time I let half of my finger disappear inside of her and she still only gives me a sheltered moan. Her muscles clench down on me, trying to keep me inside, but I still pull it out.

Cupping her entire pussy, I bite down on her lips. "I want to hear you."

Plunging two fingers inside of her at the same time I yank on her hair, she screams out in a mix of pleasure and pain.

Music to my fucking ears.

She's so fucking tight. I've had her watched for five years, so I know she hasn't had a cock in her since me. I wouldn't let anyone get that close to her even if she wanted them to.

Curling my fingers towards me, she falls against my chest with a moan, burying her face in my neck.

"No," I bark harshly. "Look at me."

Dragging her face back to look at me, I see the frenzy in them. Her desperate need for more.

"When I'm inside of you, my fingers or my cock, you look me in the eyes so I can see what I do to you."

"Yes," she sighs, and I reward her with a twist of my fingers. Gasping, she claws at my shoulders.

She tries to grind on my hand, but I pull on her hair. "No. You take what I give you. Understand?"

"Yes," she sighs again, and I reward her by pressing down on her clit with my thumb. She cries out and shudders in my grip as I hold my thumb to her sensitive bundle of nerves.

I want her so worked up and blind with crazed lust that she begs me to fuck her. That she begs me to stuff her tight pussy with my thick cock until she's so full, she feels like she'll break in two. Then I'll forever be marked inside of her.

Rubbing circles around her clit, I work my fingers inside of her and pull her hair so her head falls to the side. I lick, suck, and bite down on her exposed flesh as I add a third finger, stretching her wider. Abri's moans and gasps are driving me fucking crazy.

"Ride my hand, angel," I tell her roughly. "Show me how much you love having my fingers inside of you." She closes her eyes and moans, letting her body take over. "The same fingers that have been used to kill. The same fingers that have beaten men to within an inch of their lives." Yanking her hair so she looks at me again, I taunt her. "The same fingers that have gripped other women's hips from behind imagining they were you. But none of them were. None of them could ever even come close."

I want to see her reaction. I want to give her an out and see if she'll take it. But instead of freezing and pushing me away like she probably should, Abrianna's eyes flare as they hold mine captive. She continues to grind on my hand, unabashedly and unashamed to take what she needs.

She can have everything. I don't fucking care. I'll give her everything.

"They weren't me." She whispers the revelation, and I scratch my thumb nail across her clit, making her scream. Her pussy clenches around my fingers so fucking hard, I think they might break.

"No," I growl, licking the column of her throat, feeling her pulse jump beneath my tongue. "They weren't," I rasp in her ear, sucking her lobe between my lips.

"Leo." My name is a fucking prayer from her soul.

She knows that prayers to the devil always come with a price, though. And mine is her.

Giving her exactly what she needs, I shove all three fingers as deep as I can and stroke her front wall as I circle her clit and press down.

Her entire body shakes and shudders as she screams out her release, her sweet cream coating my entire hand and dripping down my wrist. Her scream fills the car and makes my cock swell to the point I might rip through the fabric of my suit.

Her head lolls back and I kiss the hollow of her throat. She shudders again.

When she comes to, Abrianna looks at me, and I see the moment her mind catches up with her, because her eyes turn to ice, fracturing under the pressure.

She starts to pull away, but I curl my fingers that are still inside of her once more and she falls against my chest, the sensation too much in her swollen pussy.

"Don't pull away."

Her breasts are straining in her dress and heave against me as she tries to catch her breath.

"You fucked other women," she rasps in my ear. "You pretended they were me. And you tell me not to pull away?"

"Yes," I hiss, removing one of my fingers, but continue to stroke her slowly. "I chose women who had long blonde hair, blue eyes, pouty lips, and a body I could grab on to." I make a slow circle with my thumb around her clit. "But none of them were you."

Abrianna makes a whimpered cry of pain at my confession, but still rocks into my hand.

"Stop. Please," she begs.

"Stop this?" I ask, stilling my hand.

"No!" she cries, and I keep on with my torture.

Removing another finger, I pump into her slowly with a single finger as my thumb grazes her clit.

"Stop what, then?" I goad, needing to torture myself too.

"Telling me about them. I didn't have anyone else."

"I know, angel." I slide my hand down her back to grip her ass. "I made sure no one ever came close enough."

"How? Why?" she breaths, her lips moving against my neck.

"No one touches what's mine."

"You were mine and you let other women touch you," she says, her fingers squeezing my shoulders – her body and mind fighting over what to think and feel.

"For you," I growl. "Everything I've done in the past five years has been for you."

"How?"

"Just let me make you feel good, angel," I say instead of giving her answers. In time, she'll see. But not tonight. Tonight is for us.

CHAPTER 11
Abrianna

Making me feel good? That's all he wants to worry about? I knew he had to have other women, but to tell me he searched for me in each one he fucked? What the hell do I say or do with that information?

I want to push him away and preserve some of my dignity, but a part of me – the deep part that holds every secret I possess – is loving that he couldn't find another to replace me.

I *was* different.
I *was* special.
I'm what he needs.
No one else.

The revelation has me flooding with heat, and I know he can feel it because he squeezes my ass to the point of pain.

"You need me, Leo," I declare, and his eyes darken with my words.

"And you need me," he says possessively.

Our joined declarations confirm what we already know.

We know how much we mean to each other.

We know how much we depend on each other.

We know how much we saved each other.

And I refuse to let him ever think otherwise again. He's always been the one.

I've walked around for five years in a blind daze. I thought I was living. I thought I was doing okay. I thought I was moving on the best I could.

But I wasn't. Far from it.

I was surviving. I was becoming stronger with every passing day I made the choice to get up and go do a job that makes other people live more fulfilled and happy lives.

I threw myself into the charity as a coping mechanism. If I couldn't help myself, then I was going to help as many people as I could. That's how we're able to have the new warehouse. I raised the funds through sheer force and determination, learning over the years how to persuade the rich to loosen their purse strings.

"You're mine, Abrianna," he says fiercely, at the same time pressing down on my clit and adding the two fingers he removed back inside of me, spreading them out and then curling them to stroke my front wall.

Pushing me to my limit, I explode around him again, and he grips the back of my neck, kissing me with an unhinged roughness I use to ride wave after wave. My orgasm completely shatters me and Leo swallows every sound I make until I can't take any more, and I shove my face in his neck, sucking in ragged breaths.

Breathing him in, I whimper when he removes his fingers, but he holds me tight against him, giving me the comfort I've been missing for so long.

"Mmm," he hums. "I've missed your taste, angel. It's a little bit of heaven in my mouth."

I can hear him licking his fingers clean and I press my lips to his neck, swirling my tongue there, tasting his warm skin. It's still the same. Like spicy oranges. I don't know how he does it, but it's a taste I've never been able to replicate or find anywhere else.

It's addicting.

I want to tell him I've missed him, and not just his taste, but I swallow the words. Instead, I lower my walls and let myself feel this moment. I don't want to come to my senses and have my brain berate me for what my body and heart want so badly.

I'm tired of trying to resist him. It's only been a few days since he's been back in my life and it's taken almost all of my energy to keep myself strong around him and not give in to the visceral current that runs between us. It threatens to make me internally combust simply being near him.

But when he touches me, I all but go crazy until we reach this moment. When the tightly coiled viper in me has been unwound and satiated. For now. Until she decides it's time to sink her teeth into him next.

Leo brings her out in me.

Before him, that poisonous snake laid dormant and tame. But all Leo had to do was look at me and she locked in on him, ready to strike and make him mine.

Licking his neck again for a taste, he grunts. "That tongue of yours...I've had dreams of what it does to me."

"Me too," I whisper in his ear and his arm tightens around me, practically crushing me to his chest.

"Come home with me, angel." He's not asking me, but he's also not telling me either. It's more of a hopeful statement. But I still need some assurances before I let him back inside of every part of me.

"I want to, but..." Pulling me back, Leo slides his hand up to cup my cheek, rubbing his thumb back and forth in a lulling motion. His eyes hold mine captive, and I tell him the truth. "I need to know that this is real. I need to know you won't leave me again." I hate how vulnerable I sound, but I need to know.

I see his defenses slowly lower as he lets me see into him. He lets me see the truth in his words. "I promise you I won't ever leave again. I didn't want to then, and I sure as fuck can't do it a second time. I might as well just cut my fucking chest open and let the wolves come to tear me apart. They'd all love to see me dead anyway."

"No," I say in a rushed breath. "Leo." Holding his face in my hands, I lean my forehead against his. "No," I whisper.

"This is real, angel. Always has been. I told you we had a time limit because I knew they'd come for you once they found out you were mine."

"Who?"

"Another family. The Cicariellos. They're the ones who put the hit out on my father and uncle. And the night before I left you, one of their foot soldiers saw us. I didn't know how long we were being followed or what they knew about you, but I couldn't take that chance. It was only a week since they had my them killed and a week since I took over, and I was being reckless, needing you every night."

I slide my hands around his head and lightly massage and scratch his scalp.

"I had to make it seem like you were nothing. Just a one-night stand or a fling. If they caught wind of me having a girl…" He pauses, taking a breath. "It would be my fault if something happened to you."

"Leo," I start, but he continues.

"I was a coward. And for that, I'm sorry. I wasn't the man you needed. But I didn't choose my family over you. I chose keeping you alive and safe over having to see the light drained from you. I always planned on coming back for you. I made sure you were looked after from a distance so you could live, angel.

"Then you showed up at the club and I couldn't just let you go again. I'm selfish that way. It's still not safe for you, Abrianna. I'm still dismantling their little empire piece by piece. I need them to suffer. No matter that my father was a ruthless fucking bastard," he grits, jaw clenched.

"I know," I cajole.

"You don't know," he says harshly, his fingers digging into the back of my neck. "I have obligations. Responsibilities. Duties. All of which places a target on your back for any of my enemies to use to get to me."

"I trust you to protect me, Leo," I tell him gently, meaning it.

"I don't."

"I do," I reiterate, gripping his hair.

"You always had such a blind faith in me, baby. An angel

believing in a monster." He shakes his head slightly. "This isn't a fairytale."

"It's mine as long as you're in it. I like my prince charming handsome as all get out, but I don't want some white knight."

"No?"

"No. They're too nice. They follow the rules. I like the prince who lurks in the shadows. The one who has a different sense of judgement and would do anything to keep those he cares about from getting hurt."

"Is that right?"

"Yeah, that's right. Sound like anyone you know?"

"Maybe."

"Well, maybe you can tell him that I need him to remind me why the ones who come with a warning label are the best kind." Leaning in close so my lips are only a millimeter away, I murmur against his.

Growling, Leo kisses me with a heated possession that ignites my blood and has me melting against him in an instant.

I never stopped loving him. Even when I wished with every fiber of my being that I could.

I never told him how I felt five years ago, but he had to have known. I told him with every look, and every time we touched, kissed, and fucked.

I thought he felt the same and that he was just incapable of saying the words, but it always felt like he was holding something back.

But tonight, right now, he's never been more honest or open with me, and I've never found him sexier.

I've never wanted him more.

"Take me home with you, Leo." I lick his bottom lip and he growls, bunching my dress up and gripping my ass with both hands.

Pushing me down on his lap, I moan into him, his cock pressing against my bare pussy through his pants.

All too soon though, the car slows and Alfie parks in Leo's garage.

"Leo, I need you," I beg shamelessly.

"Not here. I plan on laying you out and spending hours driving you fucking wild."

"Leo," I groan, rolling my hips.

"I can't do everything I want to do to you in this car. Not for the first time, anyway. After tonight, all bets are off for when and where I have you."

Tugging my dress down to cover my ass again, Leo takes the opportunity to run a knuckle through my wet folds, pressing down just enough on my clit to make me shudder.

Pulling the zipper of my dress down my thigh, Leo slides his hands up my body to cup my breasts roughly.

"I can't wait to taste your sweet pussy again. I'm going to lick you clean, angel. Until you scream my name and your throat is raw."

His words make my heart pound and my clit throb. I want that more than I want my next breath.

The entire way up to his penthouse, his hands don't leave my body – touching me everywhere but nowhere at the same time. And the second we enter his place, he spins me around and pins me against the nearest wall, crushing his lips to mine.

"*Ho bisogno di te.* Wrap your legs around me, baby," he demands, lifting me up. I lock my legs around his hips and I kiss my way up his neck and swirl my tongue around his ear.

Tossing me down on the bed, he grabs my ankles and drags me to the edge.

"You wore this dress to drive me crazy, didn't you?"

"Yes," I sigh as he unzips the thigh again. Sliding his hands under the fabric, he lifts it up my body, his heated eyes taking me in as he goes. Tossing it to the floor, his eyes rake down my body that's only covered in a black lace bra.

"*Così fottutamente bella*," he says, more to himself than me. "Spread your legs, angel. Let me see your pretty little pussy."

Leaning back on my elbows, I slide my feet towards me and let my legs fall to the sides. Leo's eyes flare as his jaw clenches.

"*Così fottutamente bella*," he repeats. I always loved when he spoke Italian when he's like this. "You're so wet, baby. Fucking dripping for me."

I spread my legs further, lifting my hips slightly. "Yes. For you," I tell him, and his eyes meet mine. "Are you going to make good on your promise, Leo?"

"Always, angel." He flashes me a wicked grin and drops to his knees at the foot of the bed. Gripping me behind my knees, he pulls me closer and glances up at me from between my thighs. His mouth is so close, I can feel his breath on me, making me shiver.

Leo sucks in a deep breath, inhaling my scent. He's driving me crazy.

And just when I'm about to beg him to touch me already, his tongue makes a long swipe through my pussy, from my entrance to my clit.

Groaning, my elbows give out on me and I fall back onto the bed.

"Mmm," he hums his approval, and I start to make sounds I don't recognize as he eats me like he's starving and I'm his last meal.

Sliding a finger inside of me, he sucks on my pussy lips, driving me higher and higher until tears sting my eyes. I need just a little more, but he's holding back, making me crazy.

"Leo," I sob, gripping the blanket on either side of me.

He keeps up the torture until the pressure in me builds to the point where I open my eyes and the room is spinning.

"Please," I beg, and he hums against me. Pressing my thighs down, he adds a second finger and clasps his lips around my clit, sucking so hard that white dots appear before my eyes as I shatter into a million pieces.

I think I scream, but with all the blood rushing through my head, it falls on deaf ears as my eyes roll back.

Coming to, Leo is standing above me, looking down at me with such wonder and fire in his eyes.

He sheds his clothes, and I let myself take in all of him. From his head down, I admire every dip and mound of muscle that makes up his body. It's like he's carved from marble.

Leo stands before me like an ancient Italian warrior statue come to life, and he lets me get my fill. He got bigger over the years. His shoulders broader, his arms more defined, his abs chiseled into mountains. What hasn't changed are his hips that lead to that sexy 'v' my eyes can't help but follow to see his glorious cock hanging long, thick, and hard between his powerful thighs.

Everything about him is *more* now, and I can't wait to find out if he can give me more than before too.

He said he's been chasing me and trying to find me in

other women, and while the thought of him with anyone else makes me want to scratch their eyes out, they weren't me.

And after five years of searching and never finding what he needs, I know he'll unleash the beast on me. He won't hold back, and I don't want him to. I need him to.

I need him to give me everything.

I need him to erase five years of pain, sorrow, and emptiness.

I want to be full again. Physically and emotionally.

"Keep looking at me like that, angel, and I'll be finished before I even get started." His eyes darken and his voice lowers. "And I have so much I want to do with you."

"Please," I beg, no other words coming to mind.

"Take your bra off and play with your nipples. Let me see how wet you can get for me."

He lapped up my release, but I'm already slick with need again. I can feel it coating my inner thighs. Reaching behind me, I unclasp my bra and slide the straps down my arms, tossing it to the floor with my dress.

Cupping my breasts, I squeeze them and roll my taut nipples between my thumbs and forefingers. Sighing, I keep my eyes on Leo as I pinch and play with my breasts, growing even wetter. The cool air on my pussy makes me shudder and Leo growls, licking his lips with his eyes focused solely on my core.

"Please," I beg again, moaning as I lift my hips in invitation.

Rubbing his jaw, his eyes flick to mine and then he runs his palms up my inner thighs, pressing them open.

"I already finger fucked you, ate your sweet pussy, and now I'm going to fuck you until you pass out."

Leaning over me, Leo licks my slit in one pass, and I cry out in protest when he avoids my throbbing clit. Instead, he kisses his way up my stomach and brings my hands above my head as he swirls his tongue around my nipples, sucking each one into his mouth that sends straight shots of lightning to my core.

I squirm underneath him, but he doesn't touch me anywhere but his hands holding my wrists and his mouth on my breasts.

"Leo, please. I need you."

Capturing both of my wrists in one hand, Leo grips his cock with the other and slides the tip through my folds, pressing it against my entrance. He stops there, though, and my wide eyes lock on his. I see the tick of his jaw and the sweat beading on his forehead as he holds back.

"Fuck. Me. Now."

"My angel has a dirty mouth," he says, pushing the swollen head of his cock into me. Groaning, he leans his forehead against mine. "And she gets what she wants, when she wants it." Kissing me hard, he pushes the rest of the way inside of me and we both groan.

"So fucking tight. So fucking good." Leo's strained voice vibrates against my lips.

Holy fucking shit. I think he got bigger. Or maybe it's just because it's been so long, but it takes a moment for my body to adjust.

"Look at me," he demands, and my eyes fly open to find his blazing black flames burning into mine.

Pulling out slowly, I feel every thick inch of him drag through me. He pauses when he's almost out, giving me a sexy smirk, and I know what's coming next.

Slamming into me in a single thrust, I cry out in both pain and pleasure, and Leo tightens his grip on my wrists. I'm at his mercy. He can do anything to me and I'll take it. I need the pain to know it's real. I want to wake up and know that he's been inside of me and this isn't all some vivid fantasy I'm having.

Dragging his lips down my neck, Leo drives into me at the same time he sucks my nipple deep into his hot mouth. I cry out again, feeling it all. Every nerve ending in my body is sparking out bolts of electricity.

My legs tremble as I try and keep up with every thrust, so I lock my legs around his hips, and the slight change in angle makes him go deeper and stretches me further.

He's staking his claim.

All those years ago, he erased the one other man I'd ever been with, showing me how a man is supposed to fuck and worship his woman. And now he's fucking me with a relentless drive to erase five years of being empty.

He's driving away every bad thought and emotion, replacing them with him.

Just him.

Always him.

Alternating between sucking and biting my breasts, Leo drives me closer and closer to the edge of my sanity. My cries and pleas for him get louder with every slam into me, and I don't know how much more I can take.

My inner muscles start to quiver and Leo tells me roughly, "Don't you fucking dare come yet."

"Please," I beg, tightening my legs around him.

Releasing my wrists, Leo grips my hips and lifts them up off the bed so I have no control as he starts to pound into me at a rhythm that has me white-knuckle gripping the comforter.

Each hit home feels like he's so deep in me that he's reaching my heart.

It's all too much and yet not enough.

I start begging him to let me come but he just gets a more determined look on his face and raises my hips off the bed more.

Tears sting my eyes and I want to give in, but I can't. I need him to say the words.

Growling like a feral beast, Leo's eyes lock on mine. "Now," he commands, and on his next slam in, I give in and scream, my body detonating.

My pussy clenches around him and my neck arches back as I claw at the bedding, my throat closing around my screams.

It's never been like this. This is more.

Pushing through my spasms, Leo grunts and then slams into me one final time as hard and deep as he can, holding my hips flush against him as he fills me with his release, coating my walls with his hot seed.

Remaining inside of me, Leo lowers my hips back to the bed and kisses his way across my chest and up to my lips, kissing me slow and deep.

Cupping his face, I side my hands to the back of his head and kiss him back with every emotion I've kept buried, letting them flow out of me and into him. I can feel him doing the same, telling me without words how much he's missed me.

Leo always showed me how much he cared and needed me through his actions. He made me *feel* his heart because he could never say the words.

I feel it now in this kiss. He's cracking my chest open and pouring himself into me, filling my veins with him so he'll always be inside of me. Every breath will be because he gave me life.

This is us – tied together in an intricate knot that I was never able to untangle or loosen, even when I wanted so desperately to be free. I'll never be free of Leo.

Slipping out of me, I whimper at the loss, feeling our combined releases gush out of me, leaking down my ass. Having Leo bare inside of me makes everything feel so intimate, raw, and real.

I've been on the pill since college, and never once did I want anything between us when he was inside of me, and Leo felt the same.

It's just one more way he was able to crawl inside of me and mark me as his. His come is the only to ever be inside of me without a barrier, and my pussy takes every drop like the thirsty little thing she is.

Falling to the bed, Leo tucks me close against him and I drape my arm across him with my cheek resting on his chest. He runs his fingers through the ends of my hair, and with the strong, steady beat of his heart beneath me, I smooth my fingers back and forth on his side, my eyes giving in to the heaviness weighing them down.

CHAPTER 12
Leo

Having Abrianna tucked against me, I feel her light breathing against my chest, and for the first time in a long time, I feel at peace. No bullshit involving my family or business is invading my thoughts. It's just me and her in this bed.

I couldn't get enough of her all fucking night. I lost count of how many times I took her and in how many ways.

But it wasn't just me. Abrianna offered herself to me like a meal to a starved man, and took just as much from me as I did from her.

She may be my angel, but she has a dirty demon in her that's fucking insatiable.

With that being said, I can't stay in bed with her much longer. I have shit to do that can't be pushed off, no matter that my cock is hard as fucking steel right now and in need of her warm silken pussy.

Slipping out of bed, Abri hums and curls into the spot I just vacated, shoving her face into my pillow with a satisfied little smile on her face.

Fuck, she's beautiful.

After a cold shower, I dress in a navy suit with thin white pinstripes, a white dress shirt, and a navy tie. Abrianna once told me she loved seeing me in a suit, that it was the equivalent of me seeing her in lingerie. I thought that the equivalent would be me naked, but no, my woman loves her man in a suit, and who am I to ever deny her?

"Leo?" Abrianna calls out, a tinge of panic in her voice.

"What's wrong, angel?" I ask, rushing out of the walk-in closet. Her face relaxes the moment she sees me.

"Nothing," she says quickly, lifting herself up to lean back against the headboard.

I reach her in a few strides. "Tell me."

"I woke up and you weren't here. I thought that..." she trails off.

Fuck.

I tuck a piece of hair behind her ear. "I didn't leave."

"I see that," she says softly, leaning into my touch. "Thank you."

She doesn't trust me yet.

"You don't need to thank me for something I promised you."

Blinking those blue doe eyes at me, I want to say fuck-it to everything I have to do and crawl back in bed to fuck her until she can't remember her name.

Her eyes move from mine and flare when they rove over my body.

"Baby, you can't look at me like that if you expect me to go to work and get anything done."

"Maybe I don't expect that," she says, sliding her hand up my forearm. "And go to work?" She smiles. "You make it sound like you're just going into the office like a regular businessman."

My lips twitch as I fight the urge to smile. I don't even know the last time I smiled. Probably a week before I left her. She's the only one to ever make me smile since I was a naïve little kid.

After my tenth birthday, I was no longer an innocent kid playing with his brothers. I was the son of the most powerful and ruthless mob boss on the East Coast.

My life was never mine, and it will never be mine. I accepted that a long time ago, knowing my fate was already decided for me when I was born. It was only a ticking clock that separated me from falling into line as the first-born son of Michael Carfano.

"I am a businessman, angel. I just have a very diverse portfolio."

Her smile grows. "Whatever you say, Leo."

"If it's whatever I say, then I say I'll pick you up after work."

"Then what?"

"Then I'll bring you back here and we'll have a repeat of last night."

Her eyes get a little hazy and her lips part as a pink flush slowly creeps into her cheeks.

"I'm going to assume by that look on your face that you're in agreeance with that plan?"

"Yes," she sighs, and I capture her lips with my own. "See you tonight, then. Alfie is waiting in the hall to take you to work whenever you're ready."

"Don't you need him?"

"You worried about me, angel?"

"Of course I am," she says, and I kiss her hard and fast.

"Alfie is going to take you. I have someone else for the day."

"As long as you're protected."

"I can handle myself. It's you I need to have protected."

"Maybe I want to be able to protect myself, too. You could even teach me."

My lips twitch again, and Abri runs her finger around my lips. "Can you smile for me?" she whispers, her voice so soft and sexy I can't help but give her what she wants.

It's a foreign feeling, but it's easy with her.

"There it is." Her delicate fingers continue to trace my lips.

"I have a reputation, angel. I only smile for you," I confess, wanting her to know.

"Good." Abri pulls me down by the neck, her lips like two pillows from heaven pressing against mine. Running her tongue across my bottom lip, she bites down.

Growling, I pull back. "I have to go, angel. You'll pay for that later."

"Looking forward to it," she tells me with a wink, and I kiss her hard, pressing her back into the headboard.

"See you later."

"Uh huh." That's all she manages to say, and I flash her another smile on my way out of the room.

CHAPTER 13
Abrianna

When I get into work, I can't help the smile that's seemingly been permanently etched on my face.

"Hey, Shelby," I greet, and she does a double take, a huge smile of her own stretching from ear to ear.

"Well, hello to you too. With that look on your face, I'm surprised you can walk."

Laughing, I prop myself on the edge of her desk. "He took me to dinner last night."

"And you spent the night making up for the lost years?"

"Something like that." I smirk, biting my lip. "I don't even know how I'm awake right now."

"Shut the fuck up." She laughs. "I'm jealous. Happiness

suits you, Abri. I'm happy you're happy. But if he even thinks of hurting you again, I'll fuck him up. Got it?"

"Yeah, I got it." I smile, loving that she's protective of me.

Another day of phone calls and emails awaits me as I secure the final details of the gala that's next weekend. I'm so thankful Sam is taking care of everything with our new warehouse, otherwise I'd be a heaping mess of anxiety and stress trying to balance everything.

With only a quick break for lunch, which I eat at my desk, I'm exhausted when five rolls around despite probably having drank a gallon of coffee.

But the second I walk outside and see the sleek black Mercedes waiting for me, my body buzzes back alive at the prospect of another night with Leo.

Taking a deep breath, I try and stop from getting too far ahead of myself, but it's no use. I'm falling back down the rabbit hole that will either have me pummeling to my death or falling until Leo catches me.

His arms have the capability to save me, suffocate me, or throw me back when he's done.

He says he wants me and he won't let me go a second time, but how do I know if I can trust his word now?

Alfie steps out of the driver's door and opens the rear one for me.

"Hi, Alfie," I greet, and he nods. "Man of few words?" He nods again and I smile, shaking my head.

I slide into the back and he closes the door, and I'm startled by Leo's deep, smooth voice. "He's paid to do whatever I tell him to do. And talking to you isn't one of them."

Luckily, it's dark in here so he can't see me roll my eyes.

"Don't roll your eyes at me, angel."

"How did you…?"

He chuckles darkly, and my insides twist at the sexy sound. "I know you."

Flicking on a dim light above us, Leo's face comes into view and he immediately reaches for me, pulling me onto his lap and kissing me long and languid. He's in no rush as he savors me.

"I haven't stopped thinking about you all day," he confesses, kissing his way across my jaw and over to my ear.

"Me too," I sigh, sliding my fingers up the back of his head.

Leo cradles me against him for the entire ride to his building and I cling to him, breathing him in and letting myself relax as he traces circles around my back. It's like our own private bubble where neither of us has to pretend about anything. But when we park in his garage, I reluctantly pull away and climb off of him to exit the car.

Wrapping his arm around my waist, Leo guides me over to the elevators, telling Alfie to hang back. The second the doors slide closed, Leo presses me back into the cool metal wall and captures my lips in a kiss that is the complete opposite to the one he greeted me with in the car.

This one is hard, bruising, consuming, and has me breathless in a matter of seconds. Gripping my ass, Leo lifts me up and I wrap my legs around him, shamelessly grinding against him to find a semblance of relief to the fire that's blazing inside of me before I completely turn to ash in his arms.

But from ashes, a phoenix rises, and I want to be that for

him. Strong, beautiful, and capable of rebuilding myself when things get tough.

He burned me once, and I came back to life a different woman. This time I'm burning for a different reason though, and so maybe I'll come back to life who I was always meant to be – the woman who's capable of standing strong beside the man she loves no matter what happens.

I keep my legs locked around him, kissing his jaw and licking and kissing my way across his neck as Leo walks us into his apartment.

"Oh my god, I'm sorry," I hear a woman say in a panic, breaking the spell immediately.

I jerk my head back to find a beautiful girl standing next to the couch, eyes wide and mouth open in surprise.

"I'm so sorry, Leo. I had no idea that you'd be…uh…never mind. I'll talk to you some other time when you're not busy."

Her cheeks heat and I feel mine do the same.

Growling his frustration, Leo lets me down, but keeps me tucked against his side, not willing to let me go.

"What are you doing here, Katarina?" he asks harshly.

Katarina? I should've seen the family resemblance right away. His sister is gorgeous, with long caramel and honey highlighted hair, wide golden eyes, and a face and body that could grace the covers of every magazine.

"It's not important. I'll just go."

I can tell she really wants to talk to Leo about something, so I slide my hand up his back and he looks down at me.

"She needs you," I tell him. "Take your time. I'll just go into the other room."

Breathing out a rush of air, he nods and kisses me on

that sensitive spot below my ear. "Don't even think about touching yourself while you wait," he tells me, low enough so that only I can hear him.

A shiver runs down my spine and I nod my understanding, looking up to see the flash of approval in his eyes. Stepping out of his reach before I do something embarrassing in front of his sister, I give her a small smile.

"Hi, I'm Abrianna," I say, holding my hand out for her to shake.

"Katarina." She smiles, taking my hand. "Sorry to interrupt."

"It's okay," I assure her, but hear Leo growl his disapproval, making me smile. "Be nice," I tell him, and Katarina laughs.

"It's good to see a woman not afraid to tell my brother what to do."

"Katarina," Leo warns, and she averts her eyes. "Abri, I'll see you in a few minutes," Leo says, and I take my leave, giving Katarina a parting smile of solidarity.

CHAPTER 14
Leo

"What do you need, Katarina?" I ask when Abrianna is out of sight, making my annoyance clear.

"I'm sorry. I wouldn't have come if I knew you wouldn't be alone."

Rubbing my hands down my face, I choose to ignore her implications that me bringing a woman home is such a surprise.

"Is something wrong? Or are you here to ask for your own place again? Or to travel across Europe by yourself? Or to date that asshole you met online?" Her eyes widen on the last one. "Yeah, I know everything, Kat, and none of it is happening. Especially the dating."

"There's no need to be an asshole, Leo. I just came to say thank you for my party this weekend and to bring you some of mom's bread." She points to the kitchen counter. "She went a little stir crazy without me home this weekend and our kitchen is filled with bread now."

Sighing, I rub my jaw and take a seat on the couch. "Sorry, I just didn't expect to see you here."

"Clearly," she mumbles. "She seems nice. Who is she? I've never seen you with anyone."

That's because she was only seventeen when I met Abrianna, and I sure as fuck wasn't bringing her around to meet anyone.

Our father would have scared her shitless, my mother would have sent her running, my brothers would have tried to take her from me, and Kat would've tried to befriend her like a sister.

I couldn't do that.

Things are different now, though.

I'm not using Abrianna as my escape from who I am anymore. She's more than that. The proof of that was in how hard it was to leave her behind and why I searched for her in every woman after her.

My father was right in that women are our weakness. But I'm tired of being a pussy and hiding behind that excuse. Abri is my weakness, and I'd kill anyone who tried to hurt her, without hesitation or remorse. But she's also my salvation. She's the home I crave, bringing me the only sense of calm in a storm that never lets up.

"She's mine," I tell her without a shred of doubt in my voice.

Katarina smiles. "Good. It's about time you guys found

women who are able to handle you."

"Handle us?"

"Yes." She nods. "I know firsthand how thickheaded Carfano men can be, so I applaud any woman who can hold her own to the lot of you. I like Tessa, and I know I'll like Abrianna too. You should bring her to Sunday dinner."

"We'll see. I'm not sure I'm ready for her to run after Ma says shit to her like she did to Tessa."

Her naïve and innocent eyes widen. "Mom did that?"

"Of course she did."

"Well, Tessa clearly survived. So it couldn't have been that bad."

She wouldn't be saying that if she knew our mother accused Tessa of being a prostitute and only being with Alec for his money. Because that's exactly what one should expect from our mother. She's protective of her children and perceives anyone infiltrating our family who didn't grow up knowing the unwritten rules of our world as a threat.

"I'll think about it," I tell her.

"Good. Now, I'll go so you can get back to…" She waves her hand in the air, not wanting to finish that sentence.

"Jimmy drove you?" I ask, knowing she has a tendency to slip away from our mother's house and drive around without protection.

"Yes," she sighs. "I let the henchman take me."

"Good." I nod, ignoring her sarcasm. She's still too young and innocent to understand the risks of being out in the world on her own. That's why she still lives with our mother on Staten Island. She has her own wing of the fucking mansion for Christ's sake, but that isn't enough for her. Katarina has been persistently bringing up the topic of her moving out and into her own apartment in the city so she can be closer to our cousins. They're models with an agency in Manhattan and spend their free weekends traveling and partying. So *fuck no* I'm not letting my sister do that.

Gia and Aria have their own security detail that follows them everywhere courtesy of their brother Saverio, but they're not Katarina. *She's my sister.* I would do anything for any member of my family, but she's a direct line to me, and the desired target of anyone who wants anything from me.

Standing, Kat gives me a kiss on the cheek and heads for the door. Stopping before she opens it, she turns back to me. "You deserve to have someone special, Leo. You're not immune to love just because you're you."

And without waiting for a response, she walks out. I don't move for a minute, but then remember the angel waiting for me in my bed and I stand, stalking towards her with one thing on my mind – getting inside of her as fast as possible.

CHAPTER 15
Abrianna

"I want you to teach me today," I tell Leo, sliding my hand up his stomach, making sure to savor every dip and mound of the muscles he's worked so hard to obtain.

"Teach you what?" he asks seductively, gripping my ass. "How to take my cock here?" His fingers slide through my crack and rim the tight little hole there.

Shuddering, my fingers curl against his chest. "Not yet," I whisper, and he grips my ass harder.

I want him in every way. I was too scared before, but now I want nothing undone between us. I need it all.

"Then what? Because you've got my mind thinking about only one thing now and my cock begging for this ass."

Lifting my chin to rest it on my hand, I look up at him, finding his molten eyes filled with a wicked glint.

"I want you to teach me how to defend myself. You're telling me how you want me safe, but you're relying on other men to do it. I want to be able to hold my own if I ever need to."

"You won't need to," he says angrily, his protective nature kicking into action.

"You don't know that," I respond gently, rubbing my hand over his heart to try and soothe him. "I don't want to ever feel helpless, Leo."

Grabbing my ass with both hands, Leo slides me up his torso, capturing my lips in a quick kiss. "Whatever you want, angel. I'll give you the hands-on approach." He kisses me again, kneading my ass cheeks.

Moaning, I rock my hips against his lower stomach and he groans, his hot tongue slashing over my lips. "I can feel how wet you are for me, baby."

"The hands-on lesson should start now. You don't want me handling weapons sexually frustrated, do you?"

Leo slides me easily back down his torso, leaving a trail of my arousal as I go.

Kissing his rock-hard chest, I groan when he lifts me so I'm nestled on top of his cock, flush against his stomach.

"I can't have you ever going without," he says wickedly, rubbing me against his length, my pooling wetness making it easy.

"I need you inside of me," I tell him desperately, and when he slides me up his length again, he tilts my hips so the tip of his cock slips into me, but then he pulls me away and goes back to his slow rubbing.

"Leo," I groan, digging my nails into his sides. I try and lift myself to position him at my entrance, but he has too firm a grip on my ass to let me go where he doesn't put me.

Flashing me wolfish grin, I know he takes his pleasure from bringing me to the edge of my sanity before giving me what I need.

It's a beautiful mindfuck that I crave more and more each time.

I want to see how far I can be pushed just as much as he wants to see how far he can push me.

He continues the slow torture, each time tilting me so he slips inside of me, but just as quickly he's gone.

"Please," I beg, "I can't take much more." My voice doesn't sound like my own as I beg him over and over to fill me entirely. But he just chuckles like I'm a petulant child not getting her way, and the next thing I know, one of his hands is gone from my ass, but comes back in a hard slap.

My surprised gasp turns into a moan when the heat spreads from where his hand landed, and my pussy clenches as a rush of desire floods between us.

"Again," I tell him, my eyes finding his through my lust-filled haze, seeing the heated possession and domination in his.

Slapping my ass again, I moan and drop my head to his chest. "Look at me," Leo demands, and I lift my gaze back to his.

He slides me up and down again, each time ending with a hard slap. Over and over, he drives me so wild that I know I would slide right off his dick if it weren't for his grip on me.

I keep my eyes on his, but my vision blurs with unshed tears, fighting to keep them from falling out of frustration.

"Leo." I say his name weakly, too far gone to even speak.

"Do you think you've earned my cock yet?" he replies, challenging me.

"Yes." That earns me a hard slap. "No," I groan, changing my answer.

"That's right. I say when you've earned it."

Two more slow passes along his length and my body is shaking with how much I need him. Then finally, he lifts me up higher and impales me onto him, filling me all the way up with his swollen cock.

Screaming at the sudden intrusion, I detonate around him, not needing anything else from him. His cock feels bigger and harder than it's ever been, and my orgasm seems to last forever.

Grunting, Leo holds me down until my inner muscles slow their pulsating. Then he pulls me off, flips me onto my back, and plunges back inside of me. My back arches off the bed and I claw at his biceps as he presses my knees down, spreading me open wide with his large hands.

Hearing him groan while inside of me is the sexiest sound in the world.

Both of us beyond thought, Leo takes me with reckless abandon, chasing away every demon that haunts him, and pouring them into me, knowing they wouldn't dare touch me.

Every stroke hits me deep inside, sending sparks shooting throughout my body.

The pressure inside of me builds and I need just a little more to make me boil over.

Cupping my breasts, I roll my nipples between my fingers and cry out at the zap of electricity shooting straight to my core.

"Fuck," Leo growls, his eyes watching me intently. "Keep it up, angel."

Lifting and squeezing my breasts, I pinch my tight little peaks at the same time Leo slams into me, and I shudder, feeling too much.

Every part of me is sensitive and on high alert, and if I were capable of it, I'm positive I have enough energy flowing through me to power all of New York City.

Leo stretches me open and fills me so completely with a force that has me wondering if I'll be fucked through the bed. I know he's not going to stop until he's driven me straight to the edge of the hell fires that lick at Leo's back, begging him to give into them every minute of every day. He's taking me to the line between life and death, showing me what awaits me if I give in to him.

But he has faith in my ability to save him. So when he lifts my hips and reaches a spot even deeper, I pinch my nipples again and feel the rush of fire blaze through my veins as I let go, plunging us into the fires that Leo protects me from.

My throat closes around a scream as my back bows off the bed, my inner muscles spasming and milking Leo into his own release. Roaring above me like a lion in battle, he spills into me, and the fire and currents flowing through our joined bodies comes to a breaking point as he fills me with his hot come.

Leo's eyes are so black as they bore into mine, they send a shiver of fear through me that only makes me spasm around him again, and another wave of my orgasm crashes through me.

Gripping his upper arms, I pull him towards me and he moves his hands to brace himself on either side of my head, allowing me to lock my legs around his hips to keep him inside of me.

Taking his face in my hands, I kiss his perfect lips, giving him everything I can't put into words.

He trusts me to save him. He trusts me to keep him from completely being consumed by the darkness inside and all around him. With this kiss, I carry him back from the brink and I can feel us floating away from the fire and into the bliss of the clouds.

Sliding my tongue against his, I can taste his gratitude, and my heart aches in my chest for this powerful force of a man who needs me to keep him from completely losing himself.

"Angel," he whispers against my lips, the sentiment like an answered prayer, full of wonder.

"I've got you," I whisper back, brushing my thumbs back and forth on his cheeks, letting Leo feel how much I love him. The words are there, but something still keeps me from saying them. There's a little part of me that still wonders how he truly feels, and is waiting for him to realize I can handle a life with him.

Leo lowers his arms, blanketing me in the weight of his body flush against mine. He's still inside of me, and when I squeeze myself around him, he groans, giving me another kiss that has my heart stuttering, feeling it all the way to my toes.

Untangling from each other, Leo lifts me off the bed and carries me into his spacious bathroom, setting me down on the edge of the tub. Filling it with hot water, he adds a few tablets of something from under the sink that fizzles and foams, filling the air with a sweet rose scent.

"Mmm," I hum, closing my eyes and inhaling a deep breath. When I open them again, Leo is looking down at me with guarded eyes. I don't like seeing him like that, like he's second guessing what we just did and what he let me see.

"Don't," I whisper, reaching out and taking his hand in mine. Standing, I cup his cheek and he leans into me. "Don't look at me like that."

Taking my hand away from his face, he places a kiss on the center of my palm and then rests it over his heart, his eyes lightening from jet black back to their usual dark chocolate brown.

I give him a soft smile when I see his face relax, and he helps me into the clawfoot bathtub that looks custom made because it's long and wide enough to fit the both of us. Leo steps in behind me and sits down, holding my hips as I lower into the hot water and nestle between his spread thighs.

"Ahh," I sigh, "that feels so good." I haven't had any kind of sex in five years, and a week with Leo has left me a little sore.

"I would apologize, angel, but I like knowing you're hurting because of me. Even when I'm not inside of you, you still feel me."

"I'm not complaining," I tell him. "I like it too," I admit softly, and he slides his hands around my waist and up to cup my breasts.

He pulls me back against him, as close as I can get, and I feel his hard length at my back. Leaning my head back on his shoulder, my chest tilts upward, making my nipples peek out of the water line with every breath I take.

I watch Leo circle my areolas, my nipples puckering into

tight little buds in desperate need of attention.

He groans at the sight of me trussed up with the rest of me hidden beneath the foamy water.

Leo flicks the tips of my nipples and I gasp, gripping the edges of the tub as my hips buck upward. But he's quick to pull me back against him, his cock even more ridged against my back.

Sliding his hands around my slippery skin, he runs them down the tops of my thighs and back to my hips.

"Leo," I moan, turning my face into the crook of his neck, pressing my lips to his heated skin.

He taps my thighs. "Lift those sexy legs of yours, baby. Hook each over the sides."

I do as he says, and the difference in temperature when my legs hit the air has me shivering, but also sends a fresh wave of need through me as I open myself to him.

With one of his arms braced around my stomach to keep me in place, Leo glides a single finger down my pussy.

He makes the path from my clit to my entrance, stopping to tease me with a dip inside, and then keeps going to the tight little hole I've yet to let him explore. Rimming the puckered entrance there, I tense up, but he grunts, tightening his arm around me as he pushes the tip of his finger inside.

A whimpered groan leaves my lips and I clench around his intrusive finger.

"Fuck," he growls. "I can't wait to have my dick squeezed just as tightly in there, angel."

"Yes," I choke out, the image of him claiming me like no one else is driving me wild. I know he'd make it good for me like he does with everything else we do.

Slipping his finger back out, I shudder in his grasp, but

let out a long and low moan when he moves back up and sinks a long, thick finger into me, my pussy contracting, trying to keep him inside of me.

Leo's dick is hard against my lower back, and his heartbeat is pounding strong and sure between my shoulder blades while his ragged breaths fill my ears and his beard stubble rubs my cheek.

Everything he is and does turns me on and makes me yearn for more. It's a vicious cycle of full satisfaction and needing more on a constant loop.

"Leo," I sigh, tilting my hips up.

"You feel so fucking good, baby. Warm, slick, tight, and swollen from my cock inside of you. I could spend all day and night with my fingers and cock inside of you, and it still wouldn't be enough. I need a lifetime, angel," he tells me, adding a second finger inside of me, slowly gliding in and out. "But I don't think that would be enough either."

"Leo." I moan his name, licking the spot under his jaw that I can reach, needing to be closer to him in the only way I can reach him right now.

"I know, baby. Just let me savor you for a little while longer before I let you sink down on my cock that's begging for you again."

Sliding his palm up to cup my breast, he squeezes and plays with my nipples while he continues to slowly glide his fingers in and out of me until I'm driven to the brink of my sanity with his restrained pace.

The pressure in me builds, and just when I think I can't take it anymore and am on the verge of begging him to go faster, he tells me gruffly to let go, and I do. My knees squeeze the lips of the tub as my hips jerk up and my pussy contracts, trying to swallow his hand. The only thing keeping me from sinking below the water is Leo's hand across my chest, his palm squeezing my breast in a possessive grip I hope leaves marks.

I want to be able to see the evidence of the way he makes me feel long after my body has come down from the high.

With a primal growl, Leo removes his fingers and unhooks my legs from the edges of the tub. They splash back into the water on the outside of his and he grips my hips, impaling me on his thick, erect cock.

"Ohmygod," I gasp in a single breath. Leaning back against his chest, I groan at how full I feel in this position.

Leo sweeps my hair over my shoulder and kisses his way to the curve of my neck, biting me there.

"Ride me, baby," he rasps, sucking my earlobe into his hot mouth. With his hands on my hips, I grip the edges of the bathtub and hook my ankles around his legs as he guides me up his length.

When he's almost all the way out of me, I pause, then drop myself down on him, crying out at the intensity.

"Fuck," he groans, scraping his teeth down the column of my neck. "Take me to heaven, angel."

I've never done it like this before, and when I find my rhythm, the water sloshes around us, spilling over the edge when I move faster. Leo keeps his grip on my hips tight, helping me maintain my pace.

"Come for me, baby," he growls. "Let me feel you soak my cock and squeeze that tight little pussy around me."

My inner muscles start to flutter, and with one more sink down on him, I throw my head back against his chest and scream out my release, my orgasm hitting me with the power of a damn breaking. This angle has him deep inside of me, feeling like he's reaching my cervix and pushing my lungs into my throat.

Leo grunts out his own release behind me, filling me with his hot seed and coating my inner walls. It feels as if it'll never end, and I don't want it to. I want to feel him inside of me like this forever.

CHAPTER 16
Leo

Abrianna is so fucking sexy. I don't know how I lasted five years without her.

The first time I fucked another woman to try and get her out of my system, I was giving in to the notion that it was going to be a long fucking time before I could have her again. And I kept doing it because for a short while, I was able to forget about what an asshole I was. But it would all come crashing back the second I was finished. I'd pull out and a sickening feeling would creep through me, taking root.

I'm not a good man.

I never have been, and I never will be.

I tried once, for her, but I fucked that up.

But from the moment I laid eyes on her again, I promised myself I wouldn't fuck it up a second time. I would get her back and fight tooth and nail to keep her.

She makes me feel like the world can't touch me and that what I've done doesn't matter because she'll be there – waiting for me, standing with me, lifting me up when all I do is drive myself deeper into the abyss of an unforgiving and ruthless world that would rather see me dead than on top.

Abrianna takes it all away. I'm just a man to her. *Her man.*

"Leo?" her soft voice floats into my ears and I tighten my hold on her. I carried her to bed after thoroughly washing her in the bath, and I've been listening to her light breathing for the past hour, just savoring her in my arms.

"Yeah, angel?"

"You were supposed to teach me self-defense," she mumbles, nestling her ass back against my constantly hard dick. "Not make me weaker."

"Sorry, baby," I murmur, kissing the side of her head.

"No you're not."

"No, I'm not. I can still take you down to the gym if you're up for it."

Turning in my arms, Abri blinks her big blue eyes up at me. "Yes, I am," she tells me softly. "I want to be able to take your ass down if needed."

Something akin to a laugh leaves my lips and Abrianna gasps, reaching up to run her cool fingertips across my lips.

"What's wrong, angel?"

"I've never heard you laugh before. Or seen this smile."

"No?"

"No." She shakes her head lightly. "I like it."

"I'll keep that in mind," I say, lifting her chin. "But only for you."

"Good," she says, kissing me hard, curling her little fists against my chest.

It's another hour before we make it out of bed and are on our way down to the gym I had built in the basement of my building. The first couple floors are offices for a few dummy shell corporations I use to launder some of my money, while the rest are for me and my men.

I live in the penthouse, but the floors beneath me are all apartments for my family and soldiers who need it so I can keep them close and give them a safe and comfortable place to live. There's also a fully equipped medical suite that takes up one of the floors, and another with offices and conference rooms to conduct my actual business.

Like Alec's casino in Atlantic City, my building has a basement that's not in the blueprints. Only the private elevator that has access to the floors I operate on can reach the basement. It's where my men and I come to train and blow off steam, as well as conduct any interrogations when necessary. There's a hall lined with thick-walled cement rooms with nothing more than a metal chair and a drain in the middle of the floor.

To get to the basement, even after you take the private elevator, you need to know which door accesses the labyrinth of rooms I built when I took over from my father. There's a numeral password to put in, as well as a fingerprint and retinal scanner. I always have control and knowledge over who has access to what and when.

My father trained my brothers, cousins, and I at our family's Staten Island home. There's a guest house in the back that was converted into a place where we learned to fight, kill, and both give and receive torturous punishments.

We were taught to outsmart our opponents and always be two steps ahead so we'd always have control over the outcome. And if we were ever found in a compromising position in real life, we would have the pain threshold and knowhow to endure whatever was necessary before we could escape or be rescued.

I had it the worst. My father made me stay longer and take the more brutal punishments when I would lose in the boxing ring or sparring mats. But my opponents weren't my cousins around my age. No, I had to go against my father's soldiers who were twice my age and double my weight.

It took me a while, but I powered through the pain, injury, and humiliation over and over until I was stronger and better and could anticipate every move they were going to make. It was like a sick game of chess. But I learned to play, and I learned to win.

When the elevator doors slide open to the basement, we step out and I place my hand on her lower back, guiding her down a hall to the right and then the left before we come upon the security panel. She watches as I key in the passcode and then hold my hand to the screen as the laser scans my eye.

Abri doesn't comment, she just watches with rapt attention and walks through the door before me when I open it for her.

Her eyes widen when she takes in the massive room before her. There is a fully equipped gym, a sparring/hand-to-hand combat area with mats, a boxing ring, and an MMA styled cage.

I made sure to text one of the men I have on rotation who guards this place to have it cleared of everyone before I brought Abrianna down here. I don't want anyone looking at what's mine, especially when she's dressed in her tight leggings and tank top that shows off every curve God graced her with to torture me.

"It's just us?" she asks tentatively.

"Yeah, baby. I told them to leave so you wouldn't be nervous." I also didn't want her looking at my men in a way that would force me to kill them. It's bad for business.

I'm selfish enough and man enough to admit that I want her to only look at me. Not that any of my men would dare fucking touch her or try and take her from me. That's a death sentence. They'll soon know about her and will protect her with their lives as they do for me.

Loyalty. Respect. Duty. Honor.

I expect it all from my men, and my men expect it from me. Those who aren't a part of my family by blood are still Carfanos when they're brought in by blood and oath.

If I say my woman is to be protected above all, including myself, they will do whatever it takes to keep her safe, even if they have to lay down their own lives.

"Keep going, angel. We're not starting with fighting."

"Alright." She nods, letting me guide her around the gym and down the hall at the far end.

We pass the knife throwing room and I lead us into the next one. The shooting range. Attached to it, through a hidden panel, is a fully stocked artillery room that houses every weapon you could dream of.

"I've never shot a gun," Abrianna tells me.

"Good. You shouldn't ever have to learn. But I never

want you to feel helpless. I want you to feel confident and strong."

"I do with you," she admits softly, stopping to look up at me

I tuck a stray piece of hair behind her ear as pride swells in me that I can make this beautiful creature feel confident and strong with me.

I have to push down the need to lift her against the wall and fuck her until she can't walk. Instead, I kiss her hard and quick and walk her over to the door to the artillery room.

"Holy shit," she breathes when I open the door, her eyes like saucers.

Leaving her in the doorway, I grab a twenty-two caliber handgun and a box of bullets, then take her over to a shooting stall where a new target is already hanging in the distance.

I show her how to load the magazine and slide it into place in the handle of the gun, and then take it apart for her to do it herself. She does it a few times until she's comfortable with it and then I hand her a pair of earplugs.

"Put these in," I tell her, then turn her to face the target once she's protected.

I hand her the gun and wrap my arms around her to hold her hands around the gun.

"Take a deep breath, angel. Feel the weight of the gun. Feel me around you. If you ever need to use a gun, you'll probably be scared and there will be a lot going on around you. But you need to block it all out. Focus on staying alive and the target you need to hit in order to do so."

"Okay," she whispers, her back expanding against my chest as she takes a few deep breaths.

"Now flick the safety off." I point to where it is. "Close each eye to find which is your dominant and allows you to see the target better. Aim for center mass. The gun is an extension of your hand." I take my hands away, but remain at her back so she knows I'm right here.

I don't bother with protective ear plugs because I like the sound. I find comfort in the deafening pop.

"Oh," she gasps after she pulls the trigger, not used to the feeling. She presses back against me at the force and her breathing becomes ragged.

"You good, baby?" I ask close to her ear so she can hear me through her earplugs.

"Yes." She nods, holding the gun back up to the target.

Abrianna shoots off the rest of the bullets in the magazine, and when it's empty, I'm so fucking hard, I could pound a bullet into the cement wall. I press the button to bring the target towards us, and when she sees she got two of them through the paper, she puts the gun on the counter and spins around to face me with a huge smile.

"I did it!" She beams, throwing her arms around my neck. I crush my lips to hers and she moans on impact, opening for me immediately so my tongue can sweep in and taste her excitement.

"No more practicing," I growl, spinning her to press her against the wall.

"I thought we could do a little hand-to-hand, though," she says innocently, biting her lower lip as she looks up at me with eyes full of ulterior motives. "What if I need to take a man down who's trying to overpower me."

"No one touches you," I grit through a clenched jaw.

"I know. but I want you to show me anyway. Just in

case."

Picking her up, Abri wraps her legs around my hips and rubs against me. I stalk out of there and back to the mats for her lesson. A lesson that will be less about self-defense and more about how I'll always get my way – her naked and under me no matter what or where we are.

CHAPTER 17
Leo

"Hey," Luca greets when he walks into my office Monday morning. I spent all of Saturday and Sunday with Abrianna, and after our little lesson on Saturday, I took her out to dinner at my favorite Thai restaurant, and then fucked her on the ride home because I couldn't wait any longer with the moans she kept making slurping down her drunken noodles.

I know she did it on purpose too, knowing I'd make her come twice before we even got back to my place.

She likes playing with fire and teasing the beast in me, and I won't lie that I fucking love it. My angel has a little devil in her.

Yesterday she wandered around my place, exploring every room before curling up on the couch to read a book. I couldn't keep my eyes off of her. Watching her move about my space makes it feel less empty and more like a home. It's her. She's my home. Wherever she is, is my home.

"Hey," I say back to Luca, flipping through the file my P.I. dropped off for me this morning.

"What's that?"

"Updates on the Ciciarellos."

"Anything new?"

"Not really, no–" I cut myself off, the page in front of me blurring with anger. "What the fuck?" I growl.

Coming around my desk, Luca looks at the photos and pages of notes that made me pause. "Who is that?" he asks, pointing to one of the images of Abrianna's business partner, Sam, and a few known Ciciarello foot soldiers outside of some warehouse in Brooklyn.

"Abrianna's business partner."

"What the fuck is he doing with them?"

"I don't know," I grind out. "It looks like a deal."

"You think your woman knows something about it?"

"I don't know. There's only pictures of Sam here." I flip through the small stack of him on a few different occasions outside of the warehouse. "I'll ask her later when I pick her up."

"Pick her up?" he asks, and I hear the note of curiosity in his voice.

"Yes," I clip.

"I see she hasn't tamed you much," he says with a slight laugh.

"Tame me? What the fuck does that even mean? I don't

need taming."

"You need something other than all of this," he says, sweeping his hands out around my office. "I remember how you were when father was alive and you'd sneak off to be with her. You were the most bearable you've ever been. For a few months, you weren't constantly on Alec and I for every little thing."

Rubbing my jaw, I try not to punch my brother in the face. "I didn't realize I was so fucking unbearable."

"And I didn't realize it would come as such a surprise to you." My nostrils flare as I suck in a deep breath, but Luca continues, gripping my shoulder. "Calm the fuck down, Leo. I just want you to know that you deserve her."

I clear my throat and look out the windows, not wanting to say that I will never deserve her. She's too good for a man like me.

"Now, let me see that file and see what those fuckers have been up to."

CHAPTER 18
Abrianna

"Hey, Shelby, have you seen Sam?" I ask. My brain is a little fuzzy from my weekend sex-a-thon with Leo, but I have to shake it off so I can get through the work day and actually get something done.

"No, not yet. I think he was going to check in with something at the new warehouse."

"I was trying to go there with him all last week and he kept blowing me off saying he has it handled and I should just wait to see it when it's all stocked and ready to go."

"Well, that makes sense. Right?"

"I don't know."

"Why don't you just head over there now?" She shrugs.

"Surprise him. Do you think he's hiding something?" she asks when she sees my doubtful face.

"No. Yes. I don't know. He's been acting weird for weeks now. Even before your birthday weekend."

"What do you mean, even before?"

"I told him about running into my ex and how I was maybe giving him another chance."

Her eyes bulge. "Seriously?"

"Yes," I sigh. "And he seemed hurt."

"Yeah, because he's in love with you."

"Shut up. Please don't bring that up. He told me that a year ago."

"And you think he's just gotten over it? You work together."

"I don't know. He never mentioned it again."

"Abri!" She laughs, shaking her head. "You're too cute. He's not going to bring it up again. He was hoping you'd realize you were in love with him too."

"Oh."

"Yeah." She smiles.

"That's never going to happen," I say tentatively, playing with the ends of my hair.

Shelby smiles sadly. "I know."

"I think I'll head over to the warehouse to see if he's there. I really don't want things to be awkward between us. He deserves to be happy and to be with someone who will love him back wholeheartedly."

"You're a good person, Abri. I hope things work out this time with your mystery man."

"I'm sorry I haven't told you much about him."

"Much? You've told me absolutely nothing."

"I know," I sigh. "It's just that he's a private person."

"Are you bringing him to the gala this weekend?"

"Oh, um, I don't know. I haven't thought about it."

"Do it. I want to make sure he's good enough for you." She smirks. "Now go make sure Sam isn't hiding out in our new warehouse just so he can avoid you and your post orgasmic glow you've got going on."

"Shelby! Okay, I'm leaving."

She waggles her fingers. "Bye!"

Arriving at the warehouse, I check my phone to see that Leo messaged me asking me how I am. It's sad to admit that he's practically erased the past five years this week. It must be some kind of old-world Italian voodoo spell he's cast on me that has me believing this is all real and can actually last this time.

I quickly text him back saying I'm good and that I'm just heading inside our foundation's new warehouse to see how everything is coming along.

"You sure this is the right place, ma'am?" the man with the car service asks, sounding doubtful as he looks out the windshield. I'm guessing he doesn't get many women asking him to drive them to industrial warehouses.

"Yes, it is," I assure him, tossing my phone into my purse. "That one is mine." I point to the building in front of us that has a new sign above the door reading The City's Angels, with Fleming Family Foundation in smaller lettering beneath. Pride swells in me that this is real.

"Would you like me to wait for you?"

"No, that's alright, thank you."

"Alright. Have a good day, ma'am."

"Thank you. You as well." Climbing out of the car, I head towards the entrance. Sam's car is here, but there are two SUVs parked next to him that I don't recognize. Sam didn't mention anything about a meeting he was having here.

It could've been last minute and that's why he didn't come into the office this morning, but he should have called or texted me if there was something going on.

His weird shit ends today. I miss my friend.

Squaring my shoulders, I walk into the large building and my hand flies to my mouth.

Oh my God.

It's amazing.

Tears gather in my eyes and I blink them away so I can take it all in. It almost looks like Costco in here.

The first four shelving rows are all labeled as food, and from here, I can see that each item is then labeled separately as well. The next row is toiletries for the shelters, group homes, and veteran housing. Then I walk even farther to find two rows labeled as toys and sports equipment for the youth centers, and various building supplies and tools that we use for repairs and such.

It's all so overwhelming, but beautiful to see our hard work standing proudly before me. It's a beacon of hope. Of moving forward to brighter futures for so many people.

I'm so distracted by what I'm seeing, that I almost miss the voices that are starting to filter towards me from the other end of the aisles.

I think I hear Sam, but there's a few others going back and forth as well. I don't know why, but I get a weird feeling. A creeping sensation starting at the nape of neck and crawling slowly down my spine.

I'm glad I went with my strappy flats today instead of heels because it makes it easier to walk without being heard.

Pausing about halfway down the aisle, I take my phone out and see about a dozen texts and missed calls from Leo. But whatever he wants will have to wait.

I keep a tight grip on my phone and purse strap as if the two are weapons I could use if needed. Leo only taught me how to shoot a gun. He didn't give me one to have for protection. This is what I get for not being able to resist him and for having sex instead of making him teach me some self-defense moves.

Something is wrong here. The voices get louder as I steadily creep down the toys and equipment aisle. Crouching down when I'm close to the end, I find a small opening between the packed pallets and cover my mouth with my hand to hold in my gasp.

What the hell?

Two men with guns tucked into the backs of their jeans are standing in front of Sam while another two are behind him, cracking open crates from one of our coffee suppliers from Colombia. Sam found this amazing deal where it's cheaper for us to buy directly from the farms, and coffee is one of our biggest requests at the shelters, group homes, veteran houses, soup kitchens, and pantries. We also get a wide range of fruits and nuts imported in the same shipment.

Sam handles all of the importing of our food and goods. We have shipments coming in from China too, for the sports equipment and toys we use in our youth centers. I never questioned him because he seemed to really have a handle on it all and showed me how we would be getting more for our money.

But this doesn't look right to me.

The crate is pried open with a crowbar and the men start pulling out the coconut straw packing material and tossing the large sacks of coffee into piles on the floor.

I don't have a direct view, but when the men stop unloading and knock on a piece of wood in the crate, I crouch even lower, a knot forming in my stomach.

Sam just stands to the side and watches them. I swear to God, if he made some shady deal under the name of my family's foundation, I will never forgive him.

Lifting the plywood, they toss it aside and I pray they're not about to pull out what I think they will.

My hands start to shake as I grip my purse strap and phone tighter, but it still doesn't change the fact that the men are unloading bricks of what I suspect are cocaine from the bottom of a crate that was supposed to only contain coffee grounds.

What the hell is happening?

What has Sam gotten us into?

And why?

I know I can't just stay here hiding because one of them will eventually see me, and I'm not prepared to confront any of them, including Sam, right now. They all have guns for Christ's sake.

I'm not close enough for them to see or hear me, so making sure I don't make a sound, I quickly and quietly make a hasty exit. My heart feels like it's going to beat out of my chest, but I don't dare stop in case there's more men around.

Once outside, I allow myself to take a few deep breaths before I take off running to the building next door. I round the front and keep going until I'm hidden along the side.

I suck in air, each breath feeling like fire in my lungs. I haven't run in I don't know how long, and now that I've stopped, my legs start to shake and feel like jelly.

I lean back against the cold steel wall of the warehouse, my eyes sweeping all around. There's no one. I'm both grateful for the privacy and scared that someone will find me and no one will know.

I ignore all the unread messages from Leo and dial his number straight away. I don't even have to wait a full ring before he answers.

"Abri, angel, baby, where are you?" he asks in a single breath, his deep voice giving me strength.

"Leo, please come and get me. I...I don't know what's going on."

I hear him growl in the background and then he barks orders at someone to drive faster. "Tell me exactly where you are."

"At the warehouse next to my new one in Brooklyn. I'm hiding. I don't have the address memorized yet. It's in a memo on my phone."

"I've got it, don't worry," he says, and then I hear him bark more orders.

"Keep talking to me, angel," he says in a slightly gentler tone. "Are you okay?"

"For now, yes. But Leo...Sam...he made some deal with people and–"

"I know. Not over the phone, angel. We'll talk after I have you with me again, alright?"

"You know?" I breathe, my lungs constricting.

"I'll explain everything later. I want you to stay on the

phone with me, though."

"I'm hiding behind the building next door so they don't find me." Running my hand through my hair, I try and remain calm, but I feel my anxiety levels rocketing.

It feels like an eternity before Leo tells me he's almost to me, and I peek around the corner to see four black SUVs racing through the lot towards me.

"That's me, baby. Where are you?"

"Right here." I step out from the side of the building.

I hear Leo breathe a sigh of relief and tell who I assume is Alfie to drive right to me.

He jumps out of the back and I run to him. Sweeping me up into his arms, I burry my face in his neck and breathe in his scent, letting it calm me.

"Thank you," I croak.

"Come on, angel, we have to go before they see us." Placing me in the back of the vehicle, he gets in next to me and tells Alfie to drive.

I look behind us, and the mini caravan of Cadillacs that came to get me all follow us out.

"Why so many of you?"

"I didn't know what we'd be walking into. Why didn't you answer any of my messages?" he asks harshly, and I slide away from him a little.

"What?"

"You told me you were coming here and I've been calling and texting to tell you not to."

"Why are you angry?"

"Because anything could have happened to you!" he yells, and I recoil, pressing my back against the door as I stare at him, blinking.

"I didn't know I was walking into a drug shipment delivery," I fire back. "I went to simply tour the new place, and instead saw one of my oldest friends with a group of men with guns as they unpacked bricks of cocaine from *my* foundation's coffee shipment." My eyes flash to his. "Which doesn't explain why you knew anything about it, Leo."

"The men who you saw Sam with are a part of the family who is responsible for my father and uncle's deaths. I have a P.I. on retainer who updates me when they make any moves. I've already broken down all their legitimate businesses, so now they're getting into the fucking drug game thinking I wouldn't find out. I leave that shit for the cartels and gangs, but that doesn't mean I don't know every dirty player in my city and who moves what, and where."

"I don't understand what Sam is doing," I say softly. "Why did he make a deal with these people?"

"He may not have had a choice. But don't worry, angel, we'll be finding out real fucking soon. I promise."

"Don't hurt him, Leo."

"I can't promise you that."

"He was there for me when…" I trail off, knowing Leo knows exactly what I'm talking about.

Grunting, Leo rubs his jaw, looking away for a moment. "I still can't promise you anything," he says, holding my gaze. "I put you and your safety above him." He leans in closer, cupping my cheek. "I put you above everyone, angel. Do you understand?"

His eyes hold so much sincerity that there isn't a single way I can doubt him. "Yes," I whisper, and he leans his forehead against mine, rubbing his thumb back and forth across my cheek before pressing his lips to mine in an intimate kiss I feel buzz through me like a thousand bees.

"What are you going to do?"

"I need to have a family meeting to get everyone's opinion."

"How diplomatic."

"When it's about the Cicariellos, we all get to weigh in."

"Right. Sorry," I say quickly.

"You have nothing to be sorry about. And I'm here for you, angel. You never have to worry about anything as long as you have me. Nothing and no one will touch you."

"Okay," I whisper, my heart swelling in my chest.

He may be feared by everyone who knows him. But to me, and for me, he's different. He's protective, thoughtful, and gentle. Except in the bedroom. There, he lives up to the dominant and beast of a man he's known to be.

All these years, deep down, I knew he'd come back for me. I knew he cared about me.

There was a reason I couldn't move on. Because I always knew that one day we'd find our way back to one another.

He may not have been faithful to me while apart, but he didn't have to be. I never thought he was all these years. And as fucked up as it is to admit to myself, I like that he tried to find me in other women and couldn't. That just proves to me that we were real then and we're real now.

Leo doesn't drop me back off at work, instead taking me straight to his penthouse. When there, I text Shelby telling her I ended up not going to the warehouse because I had to deal with something at the venue for the gala this weekend and won't be in until tomorrow now. I don't want her suspicious or telling Sam that I went there.

I take a seat on the couch and tuck my feet up to the

side, staring off at nothing in particular as Leo calls in his family to meet him here. He wants me to tell them everything I saw and then they're going to decide how to proceed.

When the men start to arrive, I feel a little intimidated, but I know I'm safe with them. Leo wouldn't let anyone near me if he didn't trust them.

Chairs are pulled up around me and my eyes dart around to see each of the six pairs studying me. I'm getting the feeling this isn't standard procedure. When mine land on a familiar pair, his lips quirk up in a half smile, half smirk. Nico. The man that brought me back to Leo. I guess there was a reason he reminded me so much of him.

Looking over at Leo pacing by the windows, I decide that since I'm the interloper, I should break the silence.

"Hi," I say softly, and they all zero in on me. Clearing my throat, I try again with more confidence, taking them all in. "I'm Abrianna." Each one nods at me, and I can't help but smile, which surprises a few of them. "I see Leo's intimidating look runs in the family."

Leo stops pacing and stands at the end of the couch beside me. Brushing the backs of his fingers down my cheek, my eyes close instinctively and a little sigh leaves my lips. When I open them again, I'm met with the intense dark pools of Leo's, and they hold so much he doesn't say.

I give him a small smile and then turn my attention back to the men before me who are all looking at me as if I were an otherworldly creature, taming the beast.

"Abrianna, this is Luca, my brother." Leo nods his head to the first man on the left, who strikes an immediate resemblance to his brother. "These are my cousins, Stefano, Marco, and Gabriel. You already met Nico," he grinds out, his jaw tight as he shoots daggers at Nico.

Reaching out, I run my hand down Leo's forearm and place my hand in his, linking our fingers and placing our joined hands on the armrest of the couch. Leo tears his eyes away from Nico and looks down at me, his anger clearing after a few seconds.

"And that's Dante." He looks at the last man off to the right, sitting a little farther away than the rest of them. A chill runs through me when my eyes meet his. Death. That's all I see and feel from him and I know he's not a man to ever be crossed. He doesn't look like the others, making me think he's not a blood relative of the Carfano family.

The Carfano men all look foreboding and deadly beneath their expensive suits, but still harbor the capacity for warmth in their eyes and expressions. This man is dark through and through. He has a scar that starts at his ear and runs down and across his jaw in a curve. I don't doubt for a single second that this man has killed more than he can keep track of, each one of them leaving an impression on his soul until he was nothing but the lives he took. Nothing but an all-consuming death.

"Tell us what happened today, angel," Leo urges, and I blink out of my trance from looking into Dante's eyes. If that's his given name, then it's pretty fitting and maybe even a little prophetic as to who he was to become. All I can think of are Dante's circles of hell, and which one he came from or will have to endure when it's his time.

Taking a deep breath before diving into it, I recount everything for them, not leaving out a single detail.

"Those fucking bastards," Luca spits out, his disdain clear.

"They're using your charity as a way to import their drugs. It's a good plan." Leo growls at Stefano, who doesn't seem fazed by it, and who was talking more to himself and thinking out loud than complimenting them. "I'll look into your shipping routes and manifests to see what we're working with and if they control the farms where you order from or if they intercept and repackage the crates at the port." I can see the wheels turning in his head and know that a brilliant mind lurks behind his calm and stunningly handsome exterior.

"Is this Sam someone you trust? Does he have a reason to go behind your back and do this?" Gabriel asks.

"Yes, he is. Or, well, he *was* someone I could trust. Now, I don't know. I didn't think he would do something to potentially ruin my family's name or get us arrested. But ever since he told me–" I cut myself off, pinching my lips together. Shit.

"Told you what?" Leo asks, his tone sharp.

I flit my eyes to his and then quickly shift them to our joined hands. I know I can't lie to him. "He told me he was in love with me." The air in the room turns deadly, and I can feel the energy of every man pulsing around me in waves that would knock me off my feet if I weren't already sitting.

Most of it is from the man beside me, but they all feed off of him, knowing what hurts their boss, hurts them all.

"I thought he took my rejection well, but maybe I was wrong." I look up at Leo. "Shelby told me he was waiting for me to realize I was in love with him. Or was hoping I'd grow to love him at some point. Once I...you know..." I look back down. "Got over you," I whisper.

Growling, Leo lifts my chin, bringing my eyes back to his. "Now I know I can't promise you I won't hurt him."

"I was never going to love him, Leo," I tell him softly, knowing the other men can hear me. And while I should be embarrassed, I want them to know how much I'm in this with him. I'm not going to cower from him or them. I may be someone who lives to help others, but that doesn't mean I'm an angel like Leo believes me to be. "I could never love him, and you know that."

Slamming his mouth down on mine, I momentarily forget about anything besides how his lips feel on mine. Like protection, possession, and ownership.

When he pulls back, it takes me a moment to blink out of my dazed state. And when I realize how I must look, my cheeks flame and I tuck my hair behind my ear until I can compose myself.

"How am I supposed to fix this?" I ask no one in particular.

"Let us worry about that," Luca tells me, and I look up to see the sheer confidence in his eyes. "Don't go back there. We'll take care of this."

"Okay," I whisper, nodding my agreement, and Leo squeezes my hand.

CHAPTER 19
Leo

"How are we going to go after them?" Luca asks after Abrianna disappears down the hall to the master bathroom for a bath. I don't want her to hear the specifics of what we're going to do to get this shit straightened out.

I've never just jumped right to the most obvious and quick of choices. Killing them has always been too easy of a solution. They took out my father and uncle Sal, Nico and Vinny's dad, because they wanted to take over my family's hold on the city's construction union and underground gambling rooms. Uncle Sal ran Atlantic City before Alec, and he created extensions of his high-stakes backroom games in locations all across New York City.

Before him, you'd have to go down some back alley in Chinatown where the Triads hold theirs. We use our legitimate businesses and offices to host our events, which is more desirable for the Wall Street assholes and their friends looking to throw their money around. We gladly take it.

The Triads cater more to the everyday man. But they aren't even competition right now as they're being taken over by the Bychkov Bratva family after Alec and I took out the Triads' leaders for kidnapping his woman and trying to use her to extort some bullshit deal with us.

We don't respond well when someone we love is being threatened or harmed.

The Cicariellos wanted what was rightfully mine by my father's passing, and they thought because I was only twenty-five, that I wouldn't be prepared. It was a real fucking wakeup call for them when they discovered me, my brothers, and my cousins were all ready to step up and claim our positions.

Which is why death is too simple for them.

Over the past five years, I've taken everything from them. I killed the men who they hired to kill my father and uncle. I burned down each of their restaurants and gyms they owned. And when Joey, the head of the family, saw I wasn't stopping until I got everything of theirs and then killed them, they went into hiding at their Long Island estate, locking themselves behind thick concrete walls and a small army of men with a state-of-the-art security system.

Since then, I've dismantled their prostitution business, not wanting to keep that shit for me or my family. I also took over their hold on the trucking union, which is why they've had to resort to the drug trade like a common street gang. I would let them have that, too, but not when they drag my woman and her entire family's business into it.

I think things through first. I don't act on impulse or based off of what I'm feeling in the moment. That's how my father raised me to be. He always said that I needed to be the voice of reason when everyone else was screaming for war. I had to make the *right* decisions for the family, even if no one else saw that.

"We're going to go at this carefully." I look each of them in the eyes. "This involves Abrianna. She's mine. I'm not letting anything bad touch her, especially the Cicariellos. I left her a long time ago to protect her from shit like this, but now it's come right to her doorstep."

"We've got you, brother," Luca assures me, and the rest nod, including Dante. I asked him here because he's the best hunter I have. 'The Executioner' is the name he's known as to those in my world. A walking grim reaper. He can dish out pain and death with the ease of ordering take-out.

Stefano has been typing away on his laptop since Abrianna left the room, and he looks up at me with a satisfied gleam in his eyes. He's our resident hacker, tracker, and everything in between when it comes to computers and finding information. He's rarely without his laptop, always carrying it around in a securely locked briefcase. And even if someone managed to get their hands on it and find a way to unlock it, they wouldn't be able to get into anything on the computer itself. He has military grade security and a remote self-destruct setting that can wipe his hard drive clean in the event it landed in the hands of our government or a rival family.

"I've got them. I introduced a virus into their main

server years ago so I can monitor them anytime I want."

Marco sighs. "We don't need to know the details. Just get on with it." He's never been one for patience when it comes to Stefano's tech talk. Neither am I, but I respect the hell out of him when it comes to all of that shit. I sure as fuck can't do what he does.

"The farm in Colombia Abrianna's charity buys their coffee from is run by the Cárdenas cartel. They use it as a front to grow their coca plants and manufacture their product. They ship it at the bottom of their cargo crates and have customs bribed at both export in Colombia and import here in the US. But from the encrypted messages I found, it also looks like a shipment of guns will be coming in next week, too."

"What the fuck," I growl, running my hands through my hair, pulling the ends. "Do they have anything on Abrianna?" I ask, not knowing what I'll do if they do.

Stefano doesn't answer me right away, and I look up to see him giving me a speculative look.

"Just fucking tell me," I demand.

"Yeah, they have a file on her and her family."

They fucking know about her.

"But they don't have a connection to you on here," he adds. "We have that element of surprise."

"Does it say who they plan on selling the product to?" Luca asks.

"Not in anything I've decrypted." He shakes his head, his fingers flying over the keyboard. "There's nothing here. They must not have secured a buyer yet."

"Do you think we should try setting a meeting with them?"

"Gabriel," Nico sighs. "Are you fucking serious?"

"I just thought I should throw it out there. We always look at every option first."

"No." That single word burns from my lips in a flash, silencing them. "They got their shipment of coke. We'll get them next week when the guns come in. We'll be waiting for them. We're going to make the Cicariellos come out of hiding."

Evil smiles light up my family's faces and Dante leans back in his chair, crossing his arms. He doesn't smile. Ever. But a look of anticipated satisfaction flashes in his soulless eyes at the prospect of inflicting some revenge that's long overdue.

CHAPTER 20
Abrianna

The hot water soaks my aching muscles and I breathe a sigh of relief knowing the situation will be taken care of.

I trust Leo and his family when they say they'll help me. I may be learning to trust Leo again with my heart, but I trust him with my safety without a doubt.

I hate that I need him as much as I do, but that's just my pride. I've always thought of myself as a strong woman capable of whatever I put my mind to. But when it comes to Leo, I'm a mushy pile of emotions that would take decades to sort through to figure out and label each one.

He's my weak spot. The reason for the best and worst times of my life so far. And while the last shred of sanity I've held onto since I saw him again is telling me that this will most likely end again with my heart completely obliterated and my body nothing more than a shell of who I once was, every other part of me is begging for me to let him in again. Begging me to trust him. Begging me to give him every ounce of love I possess.

When the water begins to cool, I let it drain and step out, wrapping myself in one of the fluffy spare towels on the shelf next to the sink. Squeezing the water out of my hair, I pat it dry with another towel and open a few drawers, finding one fully stocked with every product that I have and use in my apartment.

Shaking off the peculiarity of it, I take out a comb and methodically detangle my hair, wishing I had my…oh, wait. I look down and find my favorite leave-in conditioner and use it to aide in the process. My long hair tends to have a mind of its own sometimes.

When I manage to get it free of knots, I pad out into Leo's bedroom, holding the towel close to my chest. I don't know how long he'll be with his family, but I start to walk around his space, taking in every single detail as if it will give me a peek into his mind. Of course it doesn't, though. Leo isn't a man who places sentimental value on much, if anything.

His dresser is topped with a few pairs of cufflinks and a watch, as if he tossed them there before undressing.

Walking into his closet, I run my fingers over his suits, the fabric somehow feeling like it's buzzing with Leo's energy, just waiting for him to pick one of them.

He has drawers of ties, cufflinks, pocket squares, socks, and boxer briefs. Hmm. Pulling one of the briefs out, I drop my towel and put them on. Moving on to find a plain white t-shirt in another drawer, I inhale its fabric softener scent and slip it over my head, loving the feel of it against my skin.

I bring my towel to the hamper in the bathroom and then crawl up on the bed, loving how soft everything is. For a man who is anything but, he sure surrounds himself with it.

I left my phone out in the living room and there's no TV in here. Sighing, I lean my head back against the padded headboard and close my eyes. Rolling my head to the side, I see his bedside table's drawer slightly ajar, and I can't resist.

Opening it, I gasp when I see my face staring back at me. Pulling out the pictures inside, my heart freezes in my chest, and then takes off double-time.

Every picture is of me. Hundreds of them.

I lay them out on the bed in front of me and turn a few over to see that they're all dated.

Oh my God.

I find one going back as far as the week after he ended things. They're from various angles and distances, but all look to be from a professional camera.

He had me followed.

I don't even know what to think of this. But before I have time to conjure up an explanation, I hear the door creak open and look up to see Leo standing there.

"What is this?" I whisper, waving my hand over the stacks of images splayed out in front of me. "You had me followed?"

"Yes." He doesn't even look guilty or ashamed at the admission.

"Why?"

"I needed to see you. Even if it was through someone

else's lens." He walks towards me. "There's one for every week we've been apart."

I open my mouth to say something, but then close it, not even sure what to say. "Why?"

Leo walks to me and pushes my wet hair over my shoulder, his eyes flaring when he notices me wearing his clothes. Cupping the side of my neck, he rubs his thumb over the front of my throat.

"That first week I was going to follow you, to make sure you were okay, but you never left your apartment. I had my P.I. follow you then, and every Friday he'd update me and give me a picture of you. You were always beautiful, even when I could see the pain written all over your face. You eventually got good at hiding it, but I could always see it in your eyes. No matter how close or far the picture was taken, your eyes were always so empty. Beautiful, but empty. And I put that look there."

I feel tears prick the backs of my eyes, but I blink them away, not wanting to miss the emotions I see swimming in Leo's. I love when he lets his guard down for me.

"I'd rub myself raw to your picture, but it wasn't enough." He pauses, something unrecognizable flashing in his eyes. "So, I would go to your apartment while you were at work just to be surrounded by you."

"What?" I breathe, the air leaving my lungs in a rush. "Is that why you have every product I use in your bathroom?"

He gives me a small, almost undiscernible nod and strokes my throat. "But even that wasn't enough after a few months."

"That's when you went and found other women who looked like me," I whisper, the words like acid on my tongue.

His jaw ticks. "I decided the only way I was going to stay away from you was to torture myself just a little more. I'd either go out and find a woman who reminded me of you or I'd have one brought to me. I'd fuck them from behind, pretending it was you." Tightening his grip on my neck, his eyes thunder with anger. "But they weren't you. They didn't feel like you. They didn't smell like you. They didn't taste like you. They barely even resembled you. No one matches your beauty, angel."

I try and pull away from him, but he doesn't let me. A few tears escape and fall down my cheeks, one landing on his arm.

"Don't," he growls. "I'm never going to lie to you, Abrianna."

I don't want him to lie to me, but I also don't want to have the image of him fucking other women in my head.

"I wanted you to hate me," he tells me.

"Why?"

"It was easier to stay away from you if I made you hate me. I did a bunch of shit you would hate, angel. I had decisions to make that would affect my entire family and our businesses, and then I'd have your face or your voice pop into my head and I'd second guess myself."

"You're blaming me?" I throw at him, hating him a little now for even trying to use me as an excuse.

"No," he says forcefully. "I blamed myself. I couldn't stay away from you that first night I saw you and I dragged you into a world that you should never even know exists. You're too good. Too pure. Too everything I'm not."

"Don't pull that bullshit with me, Leo," I say, surprising him. "You're acting like you stole me away and held me captive while you dirtied me like some debased debutante." His eyes widen, but I keep going. "I make my own choices. Always have and always will. Don't you dare think I didn't start this with you five years ago not knowing exactly what I was getting into. If you changed because of me, that's on you. I never asked you to change. I never asked you to be someone you aren't. I love you the way you are."

Freezing, I look away. I suck in a breath and pinch my lips together as if that will make the words magically go back inside of me. I can't believe I just told him I love him, while simultaneously yelling at him.

"Look at me," he commands, but I close my eyes instead. "Abri," he growls, taking my face in his hands. "Open your eyes."

With my heart beating wildly in my chest, I slowly peel my eyes open to look into his. They're completely open to me. Two dark pools of liquid heat I can feel enveloping me, and I fall into their depths, never wanting to resurface.

I never meant to tell him I love him. Especially not like this, and not before him. If he'd ever even say it.

I once thought Leo might have loved me, but that hope was shattered when he walked away. How do you walk away from someone you love? Now he's back and telling me everything he's done was because of me and in rebellion of me, and my heart breaks even more.

"Say it again," he demands, his voice rough and raw, skirting over my skin. "Say it again," he repeats.

"No." The word is barely audible.

"I need to hear you say it, angel."

"I can't."

Growling, Leo's eyes darken. "Baby, I'm going to need

to hear you say those three words again so I know I wasn't imagining it."

"I didn't mean it."

"The hell you fucking didn't," he snarls.

"Leo, please," I beg, tears starting to leak from my eyes.

He comes closer, leaning his forehead against mine. "Angel, please. I need to hear you say it again."

I've never heard him beg before. At least not like this. Searching his eyes, I see the desperate need in them, willing me to give him exactly what he wants.

"I love you," I whisper, and he sighs, his warm breath blowing across my lips, so close to mine.

Leo slides his hands into my hair and holds me there for a moment before molding his lips to mine. Sweeping his tongue across my lips, I open for him immediately, his tongue meeting mine in a slow caress. He's tasing the words on my tongue, savoring them and keeping them for himself.

Moaning, I fist his shirt and pull him closer, the kiss transforming into something more.

Without breaking contact, Leo climbs up on the bed and pushes me back. I spread my legs, making room for him, which elicits a hungry growl from him when he feels my hot center against him.

Tearing his shirt up and off of me, he licks, sucks, and bites at my breasts until I'm squirming and moaning uncontrollably. He moves down my body, dragging his lips across my stomach. He stops to swirl his tongue around my belly button and then runs it along the line of his boxers I'm wearing.

Flipping me over, Leo grips my hips and pulls them up, forcing me to my knees and elbows. I'm horizontal to the pillows, so I grip the edge of the bed while Leo yanks his boxers off of me, plunging his fingers into my soaking wet pussy without warning.

I scream out, but Leo just brings his hand down on my ass, making me gasp and then moan.

He knows exactly how to play my body.

I hear him unfastening his belt and the rustling of his pants as he frees himself, and moan when I feel the head of his cock slide through my wet folds, rubbing against my clit.

We both groan, and he wraps my hair around his fist.

"I'm going to fuck you like I did them. I want you to replace them. I want to know it's you now. And you forever." Releasing my hair, he grips my ass in both hands and spreads me open, slamming into me in a single thrust.

"Yes," I moan, arching my back. I don't know why him saying that makes me want to give him any and everything, but it does.

I want to be his forever.

I want to be his one and only.

"You're heaven, baby," he growls, pulling out and slamming right back in, hitting a spot so deep inside of me, my lungs constrict. "You're mine." He slams into me, punctuating his words. "Forever," he growls deep, and I feel it vibrate through me.

"Yes!" I cry, and Leo's grip on my ass becomes beautifully painful. I have no doubt he's leaving his mark on me, and I want him to. I want to feel his fingers digging into me even when he's not.

"You." He thrusts. "Love." He thrusts. "Me." He slams into me, grinding his hips so I feel every inch of him.

The only thing I think about is him.

The only thing I feel is him.

It's him.

It's always him.

"Fucking say it," he rasps, slapping my ass. When the words don't come fast enough, he does it again, and the heat from his hand spreads through me, my core clenching around him, making him groan. "Say it!" he demands.

"I love you!" I scream, my fingers clawing at the bed.

An animalistic roar comes from deep within him and he starts to pound into me at an unrelenting pace, stealing the breath from my lungs and stealing another piece of me in the process.

He already marked me as his. This isn't that. This is a reclaiming. This is a reminder to both him and I that no one will ever compare to us. We're it.

We were made for each other in the purest of forms. To love, hate, touch, kiss, fuck, and belong to. Every primal and primitive instinct between humans that makes us want to toy with, consume, devour, keep, possess, and claim our prey is at work between us.

An angel and the devil.

Light and dark.

Purity and sins.

Savior and killer.

Opposites, and yet completely made for one another. Together, we keep the balance between our two worlds. And apart, we're incomplete, looking for other ways to fill the void in our souls.

But now, with our bodies joined, my heart and soul have never felt more complete.

I want to be everything he needs. If he needs to confess

his sins to me so I'll forgive him and love him despite of them, then that's what I'll do.

I would never forgive him if he did it while we were together. But apart? While he's missing me and trying the only way he knows how to cope? Then, yes, I can forgive him, because I know he'll work that much harder to earn my love and give me everything I need from him in return.

My inner muscles start to quiver with every stroke, barely hanging on by a thread. But this is for him, so I hold on as long as I can.

Everything he is and does is hard and bruising, and even if I were covered in his marks of passion, I would wear them proudly as his woman.

He swells inside of me, and I know he's right there on the edge with me.

My elbows collapse and my face falls into the comforter, muffling my moans and cries that I have no control over. Using it to his advantage, Leo tilts my hips up, and I scream at the slight adjustment. He goes deeper, hitting the spot only he knows how to access.

It only takes two strokes, and every sensory factor I have starts to go into overdrive, bordering on the edge of torturous pain and pleasure.

"Come. Now," Leo commands, and as if my body only responds to his voice, my eyes blur with tears as I let go, my pussy contracting around him as a tsunami hits me, a flood washing through me, taking every ounce of my sanity as I lose myself in the waves, drowning.

Leo pumps one more time and then he stills behind me, a deep roar penetrating my ears that were deaf to everything but the sound of my blood rushing through my veins.

I feel him filling me with his hot spurts of come, the force of it enough to set off another orgasm in my hyper sensitive state. We both groan as I milk him for everything he has, greedily taking it all.

Leo collapses on top of me, plastering his chest to my back. His hard body that's sculped to perfection feels like a blanket of strength, his weight a welcome comfort.

* * * *

Shivering, I open my eyes to a dark bedroom, pulling the comforter back over my exposed shoulder. There's a single stream of light coming from the crack beneath the bathroom door.

At some point last night, Leo tucked me into bed with him and pulled me against him, his front to my back. He held me tightly like he was afraid I'd slip away and run.

Neither of us said anything after, and worry has me tugging on my bottom lip. Hearing the faint sound of water running, I swing my legs over the edge of the bed and shuffle over to the bathroom door.

He's in the shower? It's the middle of the night…

As quietly as I can, I turn the knob and peek inside. Through the steam, I can see Leo's outline leaning against the shower's tiled wall, unmoving.

Something's wrong.

I slip inside and close the door softly behind me so I don't startle him. His back is to me, and even when I open the glass shower door and step inside, he still doesn't move.

"Leo?" I ask gently, not touching him. I don't know what kind of mental state he's in.

He doesn't answer me, so I step closer still, putting myself right beside him. His eyes are closed and his jaw is tight, like he's trying to concentrate on something.

"Leo? Are you okay?"

He finally moves, shaking his head slightly.

"Please talk to me."

"I can't," he rasps, his voice raw and full of regret.

"Whatever it is, I can take it," I whisper, but he just shakes his head again. I can't stand to see him suffering. It physically hurts.

Sliding my hand across his stomach, I feel his muscles contract at my touch, and I duck beneath his arm that's against the wall above his head. I need to see his eyes.

He budges just enough to let me in between him and the wall, and I wrap my arms around him, silently giving him my love. Placing a kiss right above his heart, I rest my forehead against his chest and let the water fall on the both of us.

I don't know how long we stay like this, but I eventually feel Leo sigh as he wraps his arms around me, holding me so my back doesn't touch the cold tiles. He kisses my temple and I lean my head back to look up at him. His eyes are so dark that I can't decipher the irises from pupils. They're just two black holes I find myself being pulled into, feeling his pain like it were my own.

"I'm sorry, angel," he croaks, his brows furrowing like he's ashamed to have uttered those words, and my heart clenches.

"For what?"

"Everything. Everything I put you through. Everything you had to go through without me right there to support you and tell you how fucking proud I am of you. Everything I'm bound to put you through in the future if you're with me. Everything I said and did to you last night…" He trails off, pressing his lips together.

"Leo." I slide my hands down his back and around and up his torso to rest on his chest. I open my mouth to say something, but he beats me to it.

"No. Don't say it's okay." He knows me too well. "You have to know I never wanted to hurt you."

"I know. You already told me."

"Not everything, angel." Keeping one arm wrapped tightly around my back, he cups my cheek with the other. "I told you what I knew would hurt you because I still know you're too good for me. I never was and I never will be good enough for you. I do shit every day that an angel like you shouldn't know about. My hands shouldn't be allowed to touch you. My lips shouldn't be allowed to tase you. My cock shouldn't be allowed to enter you. You're heaven. And I'm never going to heaven, baby."

Taking his face in my hands, I bring him down closer to me so he can see the clarity and sincerity in my eyes.

"You're who I want, Leo. Who I *need*. Even if I had a choice in who I loved, I would still choose you. But the fact is, I never had a choice. It was made for me long before I even met you. You were always going to be mine. I won't deny that you hurt me, but I also don't want to feel that way anymore. I want to be with you. Deep down, I was always holding out hope that we would find our way back to each other. Which is why I could never move on."

"You have no idea how much I fucking need you. I've never known love, angel. Until you. Which is how I know that this…" He presses the heel of his hand into his chest.

"What I'm feeling here…" He pinches his eyes closed, and when he opens them again, they're blazing down at me. I can see his love for me. He's letting me see his love for me. "*Ti amo*, angel. I love you, Abrianna. So fucking much."

"Leo." I choke on his name with tears falling down my face, mixing with the water from the shower. He leans his forehead against mine and I slide my hands to the back of his head, clinging to him. My heart is racing, trying to break through my chest to meet his.

I've never felt so full or have heard sweeter words spoken. Leo Carfano isn't a man who loves, but he loves me. He's far from perfect, but he's mine, and I'm his.

"I love you," I rasp, my throat thick with emotion.

I pull him down to my lips, kissing him with everything I have inside of me while he kisses me back like he never has before. It's more. He pours his heart and soul into me, letting me feel his words.

We stay like this, just kissing each other, leaving ourselves open and vulnerable like we haven't before.

When it becomes too much to hold inside anymore, Leo picks me up and I wrap my legs around him as he pushes me against the wall. I'm slick and ready for him, and he slides right inside of me.

We groan into each other, and breaking our kiss for the first time, I gasp for air and tilt my head to the side as Leo kisses his way across my jaw and down the side of my neck.

He moves inside of me slowly at first, until I'm panting and clawing at his shoulders.

"More, Leo," I say on a moan. "I need more."

Growling, his eyes flash with hunger and he picks up his pace, giving me exactly what I need to be quickly pushed over the edge.

My long and low moan echoes around us in the shower, and I grab his face, fusing my lips to his in a hard kiss. It only takes Leo one more stroke, and he stills, his body practically vibrating as he pours into me.

I swallow his groan, taking it and keeping it as a victory – a token to how I can make this incredible man fall apart when no one else can.

When we both come down from our highs, Leo gently washes me from head to toe, and then does the same to himself. I'm too spent to do it myself, so I lean against the wall and watch him through hooded eyes.

My God, he's beautiful. A true work of art.

Patting me dry, Leo carries me back to bed, this time pulling me half on top of him. I drape my arm across his torso, hooking my leg over his, and lay my head on his chest – never more content than in this moment.

CHAPTER 21
Leo

The City's Angel's annual gala fundraiser is tonight, and Abrianna asked me a few nights ago if I would go. She was so nervous to ask me, nibbling on her lip like I wouldn't say yes. As if I'd fucking let her go alone, especially with Sam being there.

She's somehow managed to avoid him all week, and has been working hard to make sure everything is perfect for tonight. It helped that Sam was also preoccupied with his new business friends and spent a lot of his days down at the warehouse.

He has no idea she saw him, and that fucker is still telling her not to come yet because he's getting it ready for her. That he's still organizing shipments and logistics so the transition with their delivery vans and trucks to the shelters and shit will be smooth and without confusion.

I'll give it to him, he can talk some real believable bullshit when he needs to. I've had two men following him since Monday to make sure he doesn't do anything else that will get my angel in serious trouble before we make our move. I can get her out of just about anything, but I can't save her family's name from being dragged through the mud. All the hard work she's put into the foundation will just crumble to dust.

People tend to not want to be associated with drug smugglers and arms dealers, despite the fact that most charities are fronts for some shady shit. They're just good at hiding it.

But tonight, Abrianna will have to stand with Sam as a unified front to represent the foundation, and she's nervous she'll give away that she knows what he's been up to.

I filled her in on the plan Tuesday night, and I could see her heart breaking knowing she'd been betrayed by a friend. My hands itch to kill Sam just for making her hurt like this, but I can't. Not yet, at least.

"Jesus," Luca groans. "I haven't been to one of these things in years. The food better be good and there better be a beautiful woman I can take home."

"There will be. But you can't leave early." I pin him with a look.

"I know. We won't let anything happen to her," he assures me, and I hear the sincerity in his tone.

Nodding once, I look out the back window of the SUV and watch the city blur by, rivets of rain sliding down the glass.

"Stay on the perimeter. I'll let you know if I need you inside," I tell Alfie when we pull up to the hotel where the fundraiser is being held.

"Understood, boss," he replies.

Walking into the hotel, I feel the eyes of everyone on us. I hate drawing attention. I've always liked to operate under the cloak of shadows. Which is why I stopped coming to events like these when I took over. Our father enjoyed showing off and making our presence known to those he had under his thumb. I, on the other hand, prefer the subtly of the games we play.

If you see me, it's because I want you to. It's easy to fear the boogieman when he's in the shadows. You never know if he's there watching you or not. And when he does emerge, that's when you know true fear.

Avoiding the cameras, Luca and I enter the ballroom, and my eyes find Abrianna straight away, a deep-rooted memory of the first time I saw her surfacing to the forefront of my brain.

Taking a sip of my whiskey, my eyes sweep the ballroom of the Manhattan hotel. Catching a flash of something shiny, they dart back over to see the cause.

A gold sequin dress hugs the body of a sexy little thing standing with her back to me at an auction table across the room. Long blond hair cascades down her back in waves, and I shamelessly take in every curve she has on display.

I can't look away.

She moves down the table to fix something, and when she bends over, I hold back a groan as her round ass becomes the target of every man around.

Straightening, she turns to face the room, and that organ in my chest that's only ever beat out of necessity starts to pump a little quicker.

She's fucking beautiful.

Her hourglass figure has me itching to map out her body in detail. First with my hands, then my mouth.

Well, my night just got a lot more interesting.

After dinner, Luca and I make the rounds, talking to every man on our father's list, letting each of them know that their payments are due soon.

Every chance I've gotten, my eyes have found their way to the mystery beauty who hasn't stopped moving all night. She's clearly one of the people in charge as everyone keeps approaching her with questions, and I find that her charity name, The City's Angels, is all too fitting for her. She's an angel amongst a room of devils not anywhere near worthy of her presence.

She's young, too, and yet everyone who speaks to her does so with respect, and I admire the hell out of it.

I need to know her.

Staying longer than I normally would at one of these insufferable events, I wait for the lights to dim and the band to start up before making my move.

As she makes her way towards the back exit that leads to the hotel, her hips sway with every step, calling out for me to grip and feel their power.

Easily cutting her off from passing the next table, I step in front of her, making her stop short. Wide, surprised eyes fly up to meet mine, and they're a straight shot to the gut.

Blue eyes as crystal clear as a cloudless summer afternoon stare up at me, and for the first time in my life, I second guess myself. I already know that this is the kind of girl who isn't a quick fuck for the night.

Her eyes show every emotion, playing before me like a movie I could watch all night.

My eyes sweep over her face, taking in her every feature. She's even more beautiful up close. And when her eyes dart down to my lips, she's greeted with a smirk that has her eyes flinging right back up to mine.

"Would you like to dance?" I ask, surprising myself.

"Dance?"

"Yes, dance."

"I…uh…can't."

"You just have to follow my lead, bella. You'll be fine."

A small smile graces her sexy lips that I can't wait to taste, and I lean in closer, feeling her breathing quicken as I whisper, "Even the woman in charge deserves a break. It'll be the best dance of your life."

"Okay," she breathes, that single word feeling like she just gave me something she normally doesn't.

Placing my hand on her lower back, I guide her out onto the dance floor, seeing the envious looks of every man in the room.

Fuck all of you pussies. You're not man enough for her.

Sliding my hands down her bare arms, I feel her smooth skin raise with goosebumps. I lift her hands to loop around my neck and I wrap my arms around her waist, resting them just above her perfect ass.

"Keep your eyes on me and let me do all the work," I say smoothly, and she gives me a smirk of her own.

"You don't want me to do anything?"

Taking one of her hands from around my neck, I spin her around quickly and then pull her back in, the feel of her against me like nothing else.

She fits perfectly.

Like a piece of heaven in my arms I have no right to touch.

She lets out a little gasp of surprise, her pouty lips that are painted a bright red separating, feeling my hard cock between us.

I want to know what sound she'll make when I'm deep inside of her. *I want to see those pretty red lips stretched wide around me, painting my cock the color of temptation.*

Leaning in, I whisper close to her ear, "Oh, I want you to do plenty, angel. I want you to let me peel this dress off of you. I want you to let me taste every inch of you. I want you to scream out my name when I'm deep inside of you."

She whimpers, her body shuddering against mine.

Pulling back so I can look into her eyes, I see her desire clouding over her once clear eyes.

"I've been watching you all night. Every man in this room wishes they were me right now."

"They do?" she breathes, blinking up at me. *She has no idea the power she holds, and I want to be the one she wields it on when she realizes it.*

"Yes. But don't worry, angel. I'd never let any of them touch you."

"I don't want them to," she admits softly, and the corners of my mouth tilt up.

Spinning her out, I watch her dress fan out around her calves like gold flames, then pull her close again, needing to feel her fire. She doesn't gasp in surprise this time. Instead, her little pink tongue peeks out to lick her bottom lip before taking it between her teeth.

My cock lengthens further, needing her tongue on me. She feels it, and releases her lip with a soft moan. *Jesus fucking Christ, I need to hear more.*

"What's your name, angel?"

She flutters her long, thick eyelashes. "Abrianna."

"Abrianna," I repeat, and she sighs, as if me saying her name was a gift. *A beautiful name for a beautiful angel.*

"What's yours?" she asks after a beat, her cheeks turning pink like she's embarrassed she hasn't even asked me yet.

"Leo." *I don't tell her my last name. I want her to trust me before*

I give her the death sentence that is being mine. Because I already know there is no way one night with her will be enough.

The memory is as vivid as if it were yesterday. I knew one night wouldn't be enough. A thousand nights won't be enough. I need her forever. But the fact still remains that being with me is a death sentence.

Love can't save you from a bullet or a blade.

CHAPTER 22
Abrianna

I spot Leo across the ballroom and I immediately relax, releasing a heaving breath. I've had to smile and be polite all day to people, including Sam, when all I've wanted to do is say fuck-it and go home and order take-out while downing a bottle of wine.

But I can do this as long as I have Leo with me.

"Hey, Abri," Sam says beside me. I flinch, not having realized he approached.

"What do you need?" I ask, keeping my eyes on Leo, whose face goes from semi-relaxed to full-blown shut down mode when he sees who's next to me.

"Are you okay?"

"Yes," I sigh, turning to look at him finally. "Is something wrong?"

"No. Just checking to see if you wanted me to take over here." He indicates the table behind me where I was placing clipboards down in front of the silent auction items.

"Oh, yeah, thanks." I give him a small, forced smile, and quickly duck away, walking straight across the room to Leo. He meets me halfway and takes me in his arms, wrapping me in his strength.

"You look beautiful, angel," he rasps in my ear. "Just like the first time I saw you."

"It's the same dress," I tell him. "I thought you might like it." I love this dress. That night was the first and only time I wore it, and I've kept it in the back of my closet, just waiting for the next opportunity.

"Like it?" he admonishes, pulling back to hold me at arm's length away, raking his gaze up and down my body. "Baby, I fucking love it," he practically growls, his rough voice coating my insides like warm honey.

"I wanted to be reminded of the best night of my life," I confess shyly, looking up at him. "I don't care what happens with anything. You asking me to dance was the best thing to ever happen to me."

His eyes darken at my words and he pulls me close, kissing me hard. I don't care that I'm in the middle of my own event or who might be watching. I'm claiming this man as mine for everyone to see.

"You two might want to keep this shit PG-13," a deep voice says with a dark chuckle, and I pull away to see Luca standing beside Leo, smirking. "Hey, Abrianna."

"Hi, Luca," I reply, feeling my cheeks heat.

Leo grunts. "Ignore him."

"No, he's right. I just tend to forget where I am with you."

"That's my goal, angel." He smirks, tucking me against his side. "Where are we sitting tonight?"

Blinking out of my dazed state, I look around us and then point to the front table. "We're over there."

"Me too?" Luca asks, and I smile.

"Of course. I wouldn't let you fend for yourself out there with the sharks."

"Ah, I don't mind the sharks. So long as they have big tits and daddy issues."

"Okay." I laugh, and Leo tightens his arm around me. "But you're still with us if that's alright."

"Of course it is," Leo assures me, and we make our way over. I get envious looks from the women we pass, but I ignore them, holding my head high. "I saw Sam talking to you."

"It's been exhausting pretending all day."

"Just a little while longer, baby," Leo murmurs when we reach the table, kissing the spot below my ear. "Then I can slide the zipper of this dress down and watch it fall from your sexy body like I did that first night. It was the best night of my life too. The day an angel let me see and feel heaven."

"Leo," I breathe, leaning into his chest, my legs suddenly unstable.

"Just keep thinking of that and you'll make it through the night."

"Mhmm," I hum, taking a deep breath and letting my lungs fill with his manly, spicy scent that's like a drug. I'll do just about anything for a hit of it.

"Abri, honey?"

Oh, shit.

Turning away from Leo, I find my parents standing there staring at me. My mom is smiling at me and my dad is glaring at Leo.

"Mom, dad, hi," I manage to force through my constricted lungs. "I thought you couldn't come tonight."

"We wanted to surprise you," my dad says gruffly, still looking between Leo and Luca and not at me.

I let out a nervous laugh. "Well, you did. But I'm glad you're here. I'm sure everyone would love to hear you say a few words, mom."

"Sure, honey. Who's your friend?"

"Right, sorry." I laugh nervously again. "This is Leo Carfano and his brother Luca." My dad's eyes flare with recognition before turning into slits.

"I see," he says.

"Hello, Mr. and Mrs. Fleming," Leo says in his deep, clear voice, with an underlying thread of authority that never goes away. "Abrianna speaks very highly of you both." Holding his hand out to my dad, they have some sort of unspoken conversation with their eyes before my dad grips Leo's hand in a hard shake.

My parents don't know about him. I haven't seen them much these past few years, and when I did, it was only for a day or so during the holidays. It's easy to fake being happy and content when it's for a short while.

We mostly just talk on the phone.

I love them, but we were never really close. My dad was always busy working and my mom was always busy with the charity and keeping up appearances with her friends.

They're great parents, and my mom has been an inspiration to me, but I never wanted what they have. It's why I wanted to come to New York for college in the first place. I wanted my own space. I wanted to do something without having them right there to help me. I wanted independence.

And I found it all here. They thought it was just a teenage rebellion and I would move back after I graduated, but then I dropped the bomb on them that I wanted to stay and open a branch of our foundation here.

This city is a mix of those who have the most in life and those who have the least.

They were skeptical at first, but my father agreed to help me get it all up and running and let me take Sam with me, so I was grateful.

I've since learned that there was a reason I was drawn to New York. My soul was searching for its other half, and the minute I touched down at JFK, I felt that I was close to it. It still took me five years to find it, but I did.

The moment I looked into Leo's eyes and he wrapped me in his arms to dance, that was it. I felt my soul reach out to his and his to mine, and I knew right then that I found the missing piece of me that I waited my life to find.

"She does, does she?" my father asks tightly. "She hasn't mentioned you."

"Dad," I say in a rush, then mutter an apology to Leo. He squeezes my hip in response, an assurance that he understands.

"Why would you keep that you have someone serious from us?" my dad probes further, and I plaster a smile on my face.

"I just haven't had the right opportunity to tell you."

"It's lovely to meet you, Leo," my mom cuts in, taking Leo's hand after my father. "And Luca." She smiles, taking his hand as well. "I trust that my daughter is in good hands with you?" she asks Leo.

"I promise you I'll take good care of her."

"I can take care of myself, too. I'm not helpless."

"Of course not, honey," my mom teases. "It's my job as your mother to say these things."

"Okay, I think it's time I checked in on the caterer," I tell them all. Leaning up to plant a soft kiss to Leo's cheek, I whisper in his ear, "Save a dance for me."

He gives me a ghost of a smile and a small nod before letting me slip out of his embrace.

"Mom, dad, you want to come with me? I want to catch up and I'll let you have the first of the appetizers."

"Good, I'm starving," my dad says, patting his stomach, and they follow me out of the ballroom and into the kitchen.

Once the swinging doors close, my dad grabs my arm to stop me from going any further. "Abrianna Claire Fleming," he says sternly. "What are you doing with him?"

"Robert, please," my mom whispers harshly.

"Do you not know who they are, Diane?"

Her pristinely tweezed and filled in eyebrows come together. "No."

"Leo and Luca Carfano. As in the Carfano crime family."

My mom gasps. "What?"

"They're the most notorious organized crime family on the East Coast."

"Abrianna!" my mom whisper screams. "How could you

get involved with someone like that?"

"You were just nice to him not five minutes ago."

"I didn't know you were dating a criminal!"

"Half the people in that ballroom are probably criminals in their own respects. I'm in love with Leo. I have been for years, and there's nothing that'll change that."

"Years? How long have you been hiding him from us?" My mom looks genuinely hurt.

I sigh. "I haven't been hiding him. It's complicated."

"What about Sam?" my dad asks.

"Sam? What about him?"

"I always thought the two of you would end up together. I've been waiting a long time for you both to finally see it."

"I'm never going to be with him," I scoff. "And he's not who you think."

"Maybe he's not who *you* think," my dad challenges. "He warned me you've been acting weird. He said you were back with an ex who broke your heart a few years ago, and I was hoping he was exaggerating or misinformed."

"He's exaggerating," I lie, not wanting my parents to know about that. Why the hell are they talking to Sam about me?

"You represent our family, Abrianna. How could you think that being with a criminal is a good look for our foundation?"

"He's not all bad," I try and defend, but my dad just laughs.

"You're naïve, Abri," he sneers. "You don't know any better. You need to break things off now if you want to save your reputation in this city. The fact that you were just out there with him for everyone to see may mean it's already too late. I can assure you they know who he is."

My father has never spoken to me like this before. He's a tough man, he had to be to become who he is, but he's never been so cold and dismissive towards me.

"I'm not breaking it off with him. I'm a grown woman who makes her own choices."

"Not when you run my foundation, you don't."

"Dad," I whisper, the feeling of defeat starting to compress my chest. "What are you saying?"

"Your mother has worked years to make the foundation what it is in L.A., and that carried over here when you wanted to follow in her footsteps. I won't let you ruin that, Abri. Either you break things off or this is your last night working for the foundation."

"What?" I breathe. Am I hearing him correctly?

"You heard me, Abrianna. Choose. Right now. The foundation or him."

"Are you serious?" I take a step back and place my hand on my forehead, suddenly feeling dizzy. Either choice breaks my heart. I love Leo and I love my job.

Although it's not just a job. It's been my life for the past five and a half years. But Leo is my life, too. He's in my heart, my soul, and my every breath. I wouldn't survive without him. I barely did once, and I know I wouldn't be able to again.

My job, though? There's more than one way to help people.

"What will it be? The choice shouldn't be so hard, Abri."

"You're right," I say, standing up straight. Looking back and forth between my parents, my mom is looking at me with wide, tear-filled eyes, and my dad is looking at me like I'm just a problem he needs to solve. Well, I'm about to solve it for him. "And despite putting in years to make The City's Angels what it is here in New York, not to mention the expansion we just underwent, I'm going to walk away."

"Abri," my mom pleads, tears leaking from her eyes.

"Don't pretend, mom," I say harsher than I meant to. "I'm being ambushed at an event I spent months organizing and made to choose between the two loves of my lives. Well, I'm choosing the one I can't replace. Now, if you'll excuse me, I have to check on the food and make sure my event goes as smoothly as possible." Stepping around them, I walk on shaky legs deeper into the kitchen, ignoring the curious looks from the waitstaff that undoubtedly saw my exchange in the corner. I hold my head high, refusing to give in to the crushing feeling in my chest.

There will be time later to grieve. Right now, I need to remain strong.

After talking with the caterer about the pace of the courses, I walk out the other doors that lead to a back hallway rather than the ballroom. I just need a minute. But instead of finding a semblance of peace, I turn the corner and see Sam talking with the two men I saw him with at the warehouse.

Ducking back around the corner before they see me, I listen to them talking.

"You didn't tell us your little partner was Leo fucking Carfano's woman."

"She never told me who he was," Sam says, a slight waver in his voice.

"Well, this just adds to our deal. Boss will be pleased to hear about this."

"Why?"

"You don't need to worry about that."

"I do if it concerns Abrianna. We agreed she wasn't to ever be involved."

"That was before. We'll be in touch." And with that, I hear their footsteps echo away and I slip back into the kitchen, hurrying through to the other side and out into the ballroom.

My eyes go straight to Leo, who's sitting at our table talking to Luca, and feeling my gaze, he looks up.

He must read something in my expression because he says something to Luca and then stands, walking straight to me.

I have no regrets in my decision. Seeing him stride towards me, that look of determination on his face, ready to fix whatever is bothering me…it's all I need.

"What's wrong, angel? What happened?"

"Will you dance with me?"

His eyes flit between mine, knowing I'm hiding something, but he nods, taking my hand and leading me out onto the dance floor. If this is my last night as Abrianna Fleming, the one these people in the room know me as, then I'm going to show them exactly who I'm going to be one day – Abrianna Carfano.

The band is playing a slow and sweet melody during appetizers, and while there are a few couples out on the dance floor, it feels like it's just Leo and I.

"Are you going to tell me what's wrong?" he asks me, circling his hands around my waist.

"Yes. I just want a minute with you to relive a moment I never want tainted."

"Why would it be, angel?"

"My dad made me choose between you and the charity."

Leo freezes.

"What?" His voice drops to a dangerous level, and I lightly scratch at the nape of his neck to keep him calm.

"My mom just stood there and did nothing while my dad told me that I was throwing away my reputation and ruining our family's name and all of my mom's hard work just by being with you. So, he made me choose."

I can feel the ice cracking through his veins. I need to calm him down before he explodes.

His eyes bore into mine, and despite the crazed look in them, he's able to ask in an eerily calm voice, "What did you tell him?"

I can't help the smile that tilts the corners of my mouth up. "Leo, I will always choose you. I thought you knew that."

His body relaxes just the slightest from its rigid posture. "They're your parents, angel. This charity is just as much yours as it is theirs."

"I know. But they don't see it that way. There's more, too."

"Did he hurt you?" he grinds out.

"No. No, of course not. But when I went to have a moment alone, I saw Sam and two of the guys from the warehouse in the hall. I overheard them talking about how now that they know I'm with you, their boss is going to be pleased. That somehow their deal with Sam is even better now."

"Fuck," Leo curses. "When and where did you hear this? We have to go." Dragging me off the dance floor and back to the table, he grips Luca's shoulder. "Come with me. Now."

Without argument, Luca walks out of the ballroom with us and into the hallway that connects it to the hotel area.

"What's going on?"

"Cicariello's men are here and they're reporting back to Joey that Abrianna's mine." I can tell Leo is on the verge of breaking his calm demeanor.

"Leo," I say gently. "I can't leave the event. I have to stay until the end. My dad may not think highly of me at the moment, but those we help need the money this gala generates."

"What the fuck do you mean your father doesn't think highly of you?" Luca cuts in, clearly angry.

"It's nothing," I say, and Leo growls, but doesn't correct me. "Just let me stay at least through the speeches and then I would love nothing more than for you to take me home with you. Alright?"

"Fine."

"Good." I lean up and place a soft kiss to his lips and then take his hand in mine. I refuse to hide that I love him. My parents are my parents, but it's time I start a life that's all mine. I thought I was by starting up The City's Angels across the country from them, but I wasn't. I'm not naïve like my dad thinks, but I was mistaken thinking I could have a foot in both worlds.

CHAPTER 23
Leo

Walking back into the ballroom, I grip Abrianna's hand like it's going to stop her from leaving or from someone taking her from me. She just told me she chooses me. Above her family. Above her charity. Above everything, she chooses me.

My angel fucking loves me.

And in return, I'm going to protect her with everything I have, including my life.

What little piece of my heart in the center that's still red and warm that the evils of my life haven't turned black and cold, has remained that way because of her. It's hers. It's her piece of me that no one else will ever know or be able to steal or bargain for.

When I see her parents sitting at our table, my vision blurs with pure rage. Who the fuck do they think they are?

"What the fuck?" I growl.

"They must have asked Sam where they're sitting. We had saved two seats for them in case they showed."

"You still want to stay?"

She looks up at me. "Yes. They don't get to ruin this further for me. Can you control yourself?" she asks hesitantly, as if I'd ruin her big event for her.

"Control is what I'm good at, angel. You haven't seen much of it because you're the exception."

She flashes me a sweet smile that's tinged with the devil I put in her, and I wish I could fucking take her right here, claiming her and showing these stuffy bastards how dirty I can make my sweet angel.

I've experienced varying degrees of torture my entire upbringing at the hands and direction of my father, but nothing compares to having to watch Abrianna suffer through a dinner, speeches, and a bunch of bullshit while her father looks at her with a mix of disgust and disappointment, and her mother embodies the persona of the perfect wife, mother, and socialite.

It's fucking bullshit.

I'm glad Abrianna won't have to be a part of this world anymore. I may be accustomed to blood, bullets, and death, but at least you get what you see. This room is full of fake people who wear masks of happiness to hide the hideous shit they never want anyone to know about.

But I know.

I see it.

I could destroy any of them in a single day if I wanted to.

Luca sees it too, and he hasn't left the table, sitting on the other side of Abrianna as her second protector instead of wasting his time trying to find a woman to fuck for the night. He knows where his place is tonight.

When it's finally time to leave, Abri turns to me and places her hand on my thigh. "I'm ready, Leo," she says, but her eyes are telling me she's ready for more than just going home. She's ready to leave this all behind.

"Let's go, angel."

Without even looking at her parents, we stand and I place my hand on her lower back, guiding her straight through the back entrance and out into the lobby area of the hotel. I texted Alfie to be waiting for us, and after Luca climbs into the back row of the SUV, I help Abri as she gathers her dress with one hand and lifts herself inside. I slide in next to her and pull her close, our thighs plastered together. I'm not giving her any space to second guess anything.

I wouldn't let her anyway.

Leaning in, I whisper in her ear for no one but her to hear, "I'm going to show you exactly what you're getting into by choosing me, angel." I feel her shiver at my words, and I smile against her neck, licking her sweet skin and planting a kiss there.

CHAPTER 24
Leo

Slipping out of bed in the early morning, Abrianna curls into the spot I just vacated and takes a deep breath, as if inhaling my scent in her sleep. Fuck, she's beautiful.

Tearing my eyes away from her, I jump in the shower and then get dressed. I don't normally have meetings on Sundays, but I want to avoid discussing business tonight at dinner. Katarina planted the idea in my head, and I didn't plan on bringing Abrianna yet, but now there's no way I'm going to our family dinner tonight without Abri.

She's my family too, and after seeing her handle last night with grace under pressure, I know she can handle my mother.

Since my father died, I starting making Sunday dinner at my mother's house a more regular occurrence. Once a month now instead of just a few times a year. As much as I respected my father, I never voluntarily spent more time with him than was necessary.

But now that he's gone, I want to make sure my mother has us all around her so she doesn't feel so alone in that big house of hers, despite the fact that Katarina lives there too.

Shrugging on my suit jacket, I leave my angel asleep in bed. I write her a quick message and place the note on the counter, then head down to the conference room I told everyone to meet me in.

"What's with the Sunday meeting, Leo?" Nico asks, rubbing his forehead and taking a sip from his to-go coffee cup. "Couldn't this wait until after dinner tonight?"

I take my seat at the head of the table, with Luca sitting to my right and Nico to my left. "No. I don't want to talk business after dinner tonight."

"What's going on?"

"Last night Luca and I went to Abrianna's fundraiser–"

"Seriously?" Stefano scoffs. "I thought you swore you'd never parade yourself around like that again after your dad."

"Shut the fuck up. I did. And it was my last one. Her parents, more specifically her father, cornered her and made her choose between running their New York charity or me."

"Are you fucking kidding me? Who the fuck is he?"

"Robert Fleming. He's the founder and CEO of his own company and thinks his shit doesn't stink like the rest of them. He saw me with his daughter and decided I wasn't good for her image or reputation." I smirk, thinking about all the dirty shit I did to Abrianna last night and the way she looked so peaceful when I left her just a little while ago.

"And that amuses you?" Gabriel asks.

"Yes. Because she basically told him to fuck off," I tell them all, and they nod their approval. "She's fucking mine. And even though she walked away from everything she built last night, no one else knows but her and her parents, and I refuse to let it fall apart with this side deal her partner has with the Cicariellos. They were there last night."

"What?" a few growl out at the same time.

"Abri overheard them talking with Sam in the hallway saying they saw her with me and now they're going to use that somehow. They're going to use her to get to me." My blood starts to boil at the thought of her in danger, but I bring myself back down, needing to be the controlled and cold Leo, not the crazed and impulsive Leo she's turning me into. "We have to hit them hard when this deal goes down. No killing. Just capturing. I'm sick of these fuckers hiding like pussies. We're going to get them to talk. Then we can kill them all."

"Let's fucking do this. I haven't been this excited in a while," Luca says darkly, rubbing his jaw. He can turn it on and off. He has the ability to play the gentleman and seemingly nice guy when he wants, but lying right below the surface is a cold, conniving, and manipulative son of a bitch.

We spend an hour going over the plan we had already laid out last week, just fleshing out the details and adding a few more stipulations with the new information. We'll have men keeping surveillance starting tonight so we have a constant up-to-date status on who is coming and going and when. Then, when we get confirmation that the guns are unloaded and present tomorrow morning, we'll storm the place and seize the guns for ourselves and take the men back to our holding cells.

We know we have our bases covered because we just did a similar surveillance a few weeks ago when Alec and I were meeting with the leaders of the Triads, the Chen brothers, who were trying to encroach on Alec's territory.

On the elevator ride back up to my place, I hang my head and rub the back of my neck, trying to relieve some of the pressure that's been building up all week since I picked Abrianna up from the warehouse and saw how scared she was.

I never want to see that look on her face again.

Walking through the door, I find Abri in the kitchen, wearing one of my t-shirts and a pair of my boxers like the other night, and my dick jumps at the sight.

Seeing her in my clothes is so fucking sexy.

"What're you making, angel?"

"Oh!" she gasps, spinning around and clutching her chest. "You scared me!"

"Sorry, baby," I murmur, giving her a hard kiss.

"I was making an omelet. Would you like one?"

"Can I watch you while you do?"

"I would expect nothing less." She laughs, turning back to the stove.

Every move she makes is with a graceful purpose. I could watch her all day and never get bored.

"So," I start, when she places a plate in front of me and sits with her own across the island from me, "tonight is Sunday dinner at my mom's house."

"Okay," she says slowly, cutting into her omelet.

"I'm asking you to come with me, angel."

"To meet your mom? And your family?"

I place my fork down and look her straight in the eyes. "Yes."

Abrianna blinks. I can see the wheels in her brain turning at the meaning of what I'm telling her. Meeting my mother isn't a casual thing. The only woman she's ever met of her son's was a few weeks ago when Alec brought Tessa to dinner, and she didn't exactly welcome her with open arms.

"I would like that," she finally says, and I give her a curt nod, picking my fork back up.

"Baby, this is fucking good," I tell her after my next bite.

"Thank you." She smiles shyly, her cheeks heating. It still amazes me that she can show such innocence and shyness when I've seen her at her most vulnerable and dirtiest of moments that *should* make her blush, but instead has her begging for more like the goddess she is.

I want to see if I can make her blush even when she's eighty and I've done every filthy thing I could possibly dream of doing to her and with her. I hope she still does. I hope she still looks at me like I'm the one who holds the key to everything.

I just want her.

Forever.

For as long as I'm alive, I'm going to be making sure the angel sitting across from me right now is taken care of and never wants for anything.

* * * *

"How do I look?" Abri asks, finally emerging after spending an hour in the bathroom doing whatever the fuck it is women do.

"Angel, you're always beautiful."

"Thank you, but I want to know if I look okay for your mom."

Standing, I wrap my arms around her and she tilts her head back to look up at me, her clear blue eyes shining.

"Yes, angel. You're perfect. But you don't need me to tell you that."

"Doesn't mean I don't like hearing it." She smiles coyly, and my lips turn up in a smile of their own.

"I'll tell you every day, then."

"Good," she says, throwing her arms around my neck and pulling me down for a kiss that has me going rock solid in two seconds.

"Baby," I murmur against her lips. "I can't go to my Ma's house with my cock trying to bust free.

A light, musical laugh floats into my ears and I look down into Abri's dancing eyes.

"Don't worry, I'll take care of you on the way."

"Let's go," I growl, all but pushing her towards the door.

And take care of me she did. There was some standstill traffic on the way to Staten Island, and it's a good fucking thing I have tinted windows, because I wouldn't want anyone getting a glimpse of my little angel sucking me off like a fucking pro.

I pull up to the large white brick house in Todt Hill that my grandfather bought for my Nonna when she was tired of living in the city, and Abri sucks in a sharp breath. It can be intimidating at first glance, but it's just a house. A big house filled with too many memories I hate thinking about.

After my Nonna passed of cancer, my grandfather

followed not too long after. He was the only man I ever saw in love in my family. He was a tough motherfucker. He's the one who raised my father after all. But with my Nonna, he was different. You could see the ice melt inside of him whenever she was in the room.

Walking up the stone steps, Abri squeezes my hand in a vice-like grip and I step in front of her at the door. "I'm here, angel. I've got you. I won't leave your side."

"Okay." She nods, but I don't like seeing the little furrow in her brow. Tilting her chin up, I kiss her long and deep, only pulling away after I feel her melt into me.

Looking down at her glazed over face, I fight a smug smile and pull her into the house. She's much more pliant now.

"You did that on purpose."

"Of course I did. You feel better?"

"Much," she sighs, and I don't try and fight my smile this time. Which is the exact moment I walk into the dining room and everyone goes quiet.

"What the fuck is wrong with your face, Leo?" My uncle Tony asks.

I wipe the smile away and clear my throat. "Nothing. Hey, Ma." Leaning down to kiss her cheek, she cups mine and holds me against her.

"Who is the woman making my oldest son smile? I haven't seen you do that since you were a boy."

"Her name is Abrianna."

Pulling away, she pushes me to the side and stands. "Abrianna. It's nice to meet you." Holding her hand out, Abri takes it in hers and gives my mother one of her beautiful smiles. She could solve world issues with a single fucking smile.

"Hi, Mrs. Carfano. It's nice to meet you as well. Thank you for having me tonight."

"Of course. Please, have a seat right here." She motions to the empty chair beside her. "I'd like to get to know you."

Fuck.

"Ma," I warn in a cool tone, and she lifts her sharp eyes to mine. I won't let her interrogate Abri, but it's her house, and this is why I brought her here.

Taking the seat beside her, across from my uncle Tony and aunt Frankie, Abrianna places her hand on my thigh and looks at me, silently telling me she's got this.

"So, Abrianna. How did you meet my son?"

"We met a few years ago at my first charity event. He asked me to dance."

Her eyes widen slightly. "He did?"

"Yes. And I was surprised by how good he was." Abri laughs lightly.

"I taught him that," my Ma tells her. I remember her teaching my brothers and I for the parties my grandfather used to host back in the day when we were able to throw our money around without the FBI constantly on our asses.

We'd stand on her feet and she'd take us around the living room, telling us that we would thank her someday.

She always said a man should have many talents.

It's one of the last memories I have of my mother being somewhat happy. When her kids were still just that, kids. When we were able to run and play and were completely unaware that our futures were already laid out for us whether we wanted it or not.

"Well, thank you, then." Abri smiles.

"If you met my son years ago, why am I just meeting you now?" I hear the accusatory tone in her question and I open my mouth to say something, but Abri squeezes my thigh, silencing me.

"We didn't see each other for a long time. We only reconnected recently."

"You said *your* charity event?"

"Yes, my family's foundation has a charity called The City's Angels, and I headed up and ran the New York office. My mother runs the Los Angeles office."

"I've heard of it. You do good work."

"Thank you." Abri smiles, blushing at the compliment.

"You used the past tense, though." Fuck. She doesn't miss much.

Abrianna stiffens, and my eyes flit around the table to see that everyone is listening in. "Yes, I did. Last night's event was my last."

My mother tilts her head subtly. "Hmm," she hums, but leaves it at that. I know she'll be probing about that later, but my aunt Teresa comes out of the kitchen with a dish of pasta, announcing that everything is ready.

My cousins, Elena, Aria, Gia, and Mia all get up and go help bring out the rest of the food, while the rest of my aunts and uncles take their seats.

Dinner goes by without any more questions from my mother, and Abri gets an approving look when she offers to help clear the table.

"She's quite beautiful, Leo," Ma says when Abri gets up with the other women.

"Yes, I know."

"And she comes from a good family."

"They're not a good family," I growl, making her flinch. I never use that tone around her.

"Why?"

"It's not something you have to worry about," I tell her, but she pins me with a glare.

"Don't act like I'm some fragile old woman."

"I know you're not, Ma. Trust me. It's just not my place to tell you. She's fine, though. I'm taking care of it for her."

"Good." She nods. "I hope it all works out."

I don't know why she gave Tessa such a hard time and not Abrianna, but I don't have the energy to question it, or her. My mind needs to stay focused on tomorrow and making sure Abri is safe.

"You'll be okay?" I ask Abrianna after dessert.

"Of course," she assures me. "Don't worry so much."

"Not going to happen, angel," I mutter as I stand up.

I didn't want to discuss business tonight, but I need to fill my uncles in on what's going on. They may not be involved in the day-to-day aspects of everything since I took over, having stepped aside to let the next generation take the reins, but they still need to be aware of our operations.

"What's going on, Leo?" my uncle Tony asks, taking a seat in one of the leather chairs by the fireplace in my father's old office. He pulls a cigar from the box on the table in front of him and holds it to his nose, inhaling the length of it.

"I wanted to fill you in on something going down tomorrow. It's short notice, but we have it all planned out."

"Plans don't always work out, Leo," my uncle Richie says, taking the seat beside Tony.

"I know." I nod. "But we've got every angle covered." As my underboss, Luca joins me, sitting in the chair in front of my father's old desk while I sit behind it, feeling his residual presence.

My uncle Carmine stands silently in the corner, observing until he deems it necessary to speak. He married into the family. An arranged marriage by my grandfather to his only daughter. He's the fourth son to his father, Giuseppe Antonucci, who is still the head of the Antonucci family even at his advanced age. Carmine was expendable to him when he wanted to broker a deal with our family.

The Antonuccis wanted to get in our good graces and be able to call on us when they needed a favor, and my grandfather wanted the majority stakes they held in a steel company. It's all about give and take to keep the peace amongst the five families.

But the Cicariellos fucked all that up but murdering my father and uncle, and their day is coming soon. Starting with tomorrow.

"What's going on?" Tony repeats.

"The Cicariellos have been using Abrianna's charity to smuggle in drugs and guns. She found out her partner was dirty last week, and then last night she heard their men talking about how they were going to use the fact that she's with me to their advantage."

I meet the eyes of every man in the room.

"They have a shipment of guns coming in tomorrow and we're going to take it, and them."

"Are you going? What about Abrianna?" Richie asks.

"I'm going to have Dante watching her. I know no one will get through him if they try to go after her while we're at the warehouse seizing their shit."

"Good." He nods.

Dante isn't family by blood, but I trust him with my life, and more importantly, Abrianna's life. My father brought him home one day and told my brothers and I that he was going to train with us and be an asset to our family.

An asset is a fucking understatement.

"Shouldn't he be with you?"

"No, I'll have plenty of men. They don't know we know, so it should only be two to four men like last week's shipment. But I'm prepared for more. We're going to use them to get to Joey."

"Finally," Tony growls. "I agreed with your slow destruction, but I want to see that fucker pay. I want to make him bleed."

"We'll all get our turns," Luca says, his words making Carmine stir in the corner for the first time – a dark smile lifting the corners of his mouth.

"I'll let you know when I have them." Standing, I button my suit jacket and stride out of the office with Luca, leaving my uncles to their cigars and scotch.

CHAPTER 25
Abrianna

We make it back to Leo's place, and I feel the heaviness of this weekend and tomorrow on my shoulders. It's all a swirl of betrayal, disappointment, and confusion.

But the one clear thing in all of this is Leo. He's shown me nothing but loyalty and that he really is in this with me.

There may be a piece of me that still has a twinge of doubt, but that's only because I'm so in love with him, and I'm still wondering how he can feel the same about me.

He was made to rule. To conquer. To destroy. To survive. And I'm just a girl from California who grew up in a sheltered bubble of wealth and innocence.

"What are you thinking so hard about, angel?" Leo asks

in the elevator ride up from the garage.

"Everything," I sigh, and he pulls me flush against him.

"Stop, baby. I got this covered for you."

"I can't stop. It just feels like the world is spinning while I stand in the middle trying not to get pulled apart."

Leo's eyes are dark and penetrating as he searches mine.

"But you're there," I whisper. "You're the only thing keeping that from happening. You're my anchor in all of this, but you somehow make me feel like I'm flying at the same time."

Leo brushes my hair over my shoulder, his fingertips grazing the side of my neck. "I never knew angels existed until you. How I'm even able to touch and hold such a heavenly being with my hands is something I'll never understand. But I'm not giving you back. I may pull you into hell with me, and turn your wings black from my evils, but I promise I'll never let the flames touch you."

"I look good in black," I whisper, and he growls, slamming his mouth down on mine, taking my lips in a bruising kiss that's all heat and claiming possession. It's not gentle and it's not loving. It's ownership. And it's exactly what I need right now.

The elevator doors slide open and Leo breaks our kiss to lift me up over his shoulder like I weigh nothing at all. My breath leaves my lungs and I grip his hips from behind to keep from bouncing around as he stalks through his house. My dress flies up in the process and with one arm as a bar across my upper thighs, Leo slaps my ass hard with the other.

I cry out at the sting, but feel heat bloom from my core, needing more.

He senses that, and brings his palm down on my ass

harder this time, making my toes scrunch in my heels as tears sting my eyes and my throat closes around a scream.

Reaching his room, Leo tosses me down on the bed and I bounce once, looking up at him to see his face shrouded in a shadow of darkness.

"You want black wings, angel?"

I nod once, parting my thighs in a silent invitation for whatever he has in store for me.

I want it all.

I want every demon he keeps inside of him painted on me like art so he knows I find it all beautiful. I'll always be a canvas for him when he needs to rid himself of his past and everything he faces now. I want to look at myself and see the mix of his dark and my light swirled on my skin like a tattoo. Permanent and for all to see.

"I need to hear the word."

"Yes."

"Turn over," he orders, and I do so without hesitation.

Pulling my ankles so I slide to the end of the bed, Leo pushes me up to my knees and spreads them apart. With my ass high in the air, my loose dress falls to my chest.

Gripping my lace covered ass in his hands, he squeezes hard, slapping each cheek once and then massaging them out. I squirm beneath his touch, my core clenching, in need of attention.

Leo runs a finger over the lace between my cheeks and then presses down on my pussy. "I'm going to take you here," he tells me, and I moan at the pressure. "Then here," he says, pressing into the lace at my back entrance. I contract at his touch. "I want all of you to be mine, Abrianna. I want every hole you have to been claimed and filled with me and my come." I moan at his dirty words, wanting that as much as him. "It's going to hurt at first, but then you'll really be all mine. Because I'll accept nothing less than everything."

"Yes," I moan, pushing my ass back into his touch.

"I've only ever wanted you, Abrianna," he muses, running his hands up the length of my spine. "Since I first took you in my arms, I knew it was you. I knew you would destroy me."

"Leo," I moan, and he unclasps my bra, sliding his hands around to cup my breasts and roll my taut nipples between his fingers. My back arches and I feel him right there behind me. I need to feel him against my skin. "Please," I beg.

"Always so eager for me." Leaving a trail of kisses down my spine, Leo peels my panties down and kisses his way down each cheek. Biting into my soft flesh, I groan, my legs shaking slightly in anticipation for what's coming next.

When the lace goes as far down my legs as it can with how he has me positioned, Leo grips the fabric in his fist and tears my panties from my body – the snap of the fabric against my skin only making my need greater.

Running a finger through my wet folds, Leo grunts. "So eager," he repeats, shoving two fingers inside of me without warning.

Screaming into the comforter, I clench around him, but he takes his fingers away just as quickly. "No!" I cry out, but he doesn't respond. He just drags his slick fingers up to my back entrance, circling the puckered hole.

Leo massages my resistance away, and when the tip of his finger slips inside, he growls his approval while I choke out a scream. It burns, but in the best way possible. The kind of burn that can only lead to pleasure.

Taking his finger away, I grunt my frustration, but then I hear the sound of his zipper sliding down and his pants falling to the floor.

Rubbing his cock through my wetness, Leo groans, gripping my hips hard. He presses his thick head against my entrance and I fist the sheets by my face just in time for him to plow into me in a single thrust. A scream is torn from deep within me, making my throat raw.

"So fucking good," Leo growls out, his voice rough and strained. He holds me there, him fully inside of me, stretching me wide.

When he pulls out and slams back inside of me, the force vibrates up through me to the tips of my fingers and the top of my head. I feel him inside of me everywhere.

He takes me hard and fast, making sure I feel every inch of his length and circumference, bringing me to the edge quicker than ever knowing he's fucking me to get me ready for him to take me where no one has before.

"Come," he demands, reaching around and pressing down on my clit. His voice is all I need, and I'm exploding around him, biting the comforter to keep from biting my tongue off as my eyes roll back at the intensity.

Slipping out of me before he comes, my juices leak down my inner thighs and Leo glides his fingers through it, sliding his coated fingers up to my rear entrance. I'm still floating through my orgasm, but when he presses at my tight little hole, I tense up.

"Relax, angel," he coaxes in his deep, raw voice, and I have no choice but to bend to his will.

My body relaxes under his skilled touch, and he slips his thick middle finger inside of me like before, going a little deeper this time.

I clench around him, halting his intrusion, but he aligns himself at my pussy entrance again and slides in slowly. I moan long and low, my body not accustomed to feeling so much at the same time. He works his finger in and out of my ass in time with his cock, until his entire finger is swallowed in my most private and forbidden area.

Picking up the pace, I'm too caught up in the onslaught of pleasure to even protest him adding another finger.

I cry out at the intensity of everything I'm feeling. The burning. The pressure. The fullness. The stretching. The dirtiness. The claiming. The owning. It's all swirling together, building to something powerful and unlike anything I've ever known.

The sounds coming out of me are unrecognizable and deaf to my ears as I don't hold the capacity to focus on anything other than Leo inside of me.

Stretching his fingers apart inside of me, both my pussy and ass squeeze him, and he grunts. "*Così fottutamente buono*, baby."

With the Italian rolling from his tongue, it only takes two more strokes of him inside of me before I'm screaming into the comforter and gripping it so hard, I'm surprised it doesn't tear.

My scream echoes through my brain until Leo's loud roar penetrates through, and we both ride the tsunami wave crashing through us. My body continues to convulse until I'm drained of every drop of pleasure I have.

I'm wrung dry.

Every ounce of energy I have is gone, and I collapse to the bed. At some point, Leo leaves me and comes back with a warm wash cloth, wiping me clean with a gentleness completely in contrast to his earlier animalistic behavior.

He picks me up and places me farther up the bed. My head is still spinning, but the pillow is soft and the sheets are cool that he covers my heated skin with.

"Mmm," I hum, curling up on my side and falling into a deep sleep straight away.

CHAPTER 26
Abrianna

I wake up and Leo is gone. It takes a moment for my brain to catch up with me and realize what today is.

He left without waking me? I know he didn't want me to go with them despite my protests, but he just left?

Sighing, I dress in yoga pants and a t-shirt and head to the kitchen.

"Ahh!" I scream when I see the big scary guy I met last week sitting on the couch. He's built like a brick house and wears a scowl so deeply set in his face, that I'm not sure he's ever smiled a day in his life. "What are you doing here?"

He points to the counter as his response.

Confused, I walk over and see a note sitting beneath an

empty coffee mug.

I'll see you later, angel. Dante is there to protect you. Don't give him a hard time.
- Leo

Give him a hard time? Is he serious? The guy scares me half to death just looking at him. I won't be giving him a hard time.

"You're here to protect me?" He nods yes. "From what? Why would I be in danger here?" I look around me as if something or someone is going to come popping out.

"Just in case," is all he says. Or rather, grunts out. His voice is so deep and threaded with danger that an icy chill runs through me at the thought of being at the receiving end of that malice he seems to always carry around.

"Would you like anything?" I offer to distract myself. "Coffee? Breakfast?"

His black eyes flit to mine. "I'm fine."

"Alright." I quietly make a pot of coffee and whip up some eggs and bacon I find in the fridge. "I made extra if you change your mind," I tell him when I sit down at the kitchen island. I have a feeling he was just saying no because he wouldn't want Leo thinking I was serving him or he was finding any moment of his time here enjoyable.

The whole place is silent as I eat and Dante reads something on his phone. When I'm finished, I place my plate and fork in the dishwasher and pour myself another cup of coffee. I sneak a look at my guard for the day and see his brows drawn together as he stares at his screen. I have no idea what he's looking at or reading, but I'm not letting the food go to waste. Heating it up again on the stove, I plate it and pour a mug of coffee, placing both on the spot I just abandoned at the island.

"Please eat, Dante," I tell him, and he looks up at me with narrowed eyes. "Or not. Either way, there's a hot plate of food and a mug of coffee waiting for you over there. I figured you're a black coffee kind of guy, but if not, then milk and cream are in the fridge." Leaving him alone, I head back to Leo's room and take a long, hot shower before redressing in jeans and a flowy floral blouse.

After going through the motions of drying my hair and putting a little concealer under my eyes and mascara on my lashes, I head back out to the living room. I know Leo wouldn't have left Dante here if he didn't trust him, and so there's no reason for me to feel as if I need to hide or avoid him. Despite the fact that when his eyes are on me, they make me feel cold, as if he can see way more about me than I'd like.

I smile to myself when I see the plate of food and coffee are gone, and take a seat on one of the plush leather chairs opposite to where Dante is sitting. Sharing a couch with him, even at opposing ends, is still too close. He wears an invisible shield around him that screams 'back-off.'

His eyes are glued to his phone still, and I'm curious about what has his rapt attention, but I don't dare ask.

"Is it all right if I put the TV on? I don't want to bother you." His sharp eyes meet mine, nodding once.

And so this is how we spend the next few hours – him on his phone and me mindlessly watching TV while I wait to hear from Leo. I've checked my phone obsessively every few minutes, but there's still nothing, and I sure as hell am not asking my companion. I know he wouldn't tell me anyway.

"Boss will be here in ten minutes," Dante tells me gruffly, startling me. Standing, he starts to pace the length of the living room. The wall of windows provides a view of endless skyscrapers, but even they don't look like they'd be able to cage the beast stalking back and forth in front of them.

I check my phone, but he hasn't messaged me. The gnawing feeling in my gut I've had since I woke up amplifies, and I know something is wrong.

Leo wants to protect me from everything bad in the world, but I don't need him to do that. And if anyone gets hurt because he's on some mission to keep me safe, then I will never forgive myself.

CHAPTER 27
Leo

I left Abrianna asleep in my bed, splayed out like the angel she is. I was going to wake her before I left, but I decided it was best to just slip away so she wouldn't put up a fight or argue with me again that she should be coming with me.

Not that I expect anything to happen while I'm gone, but now I don't have to worry about her while I take care of business. Dante won't let anything or anyone touch her.

I need to choose one of my men to be her full-time bodyguard from here on out. Alec had that for Tessa before they even fucking met, but I've either been with Abri or she's been in my house whenever she hasn't been at work.

I still had my P.I. on her, but he was there to watch and monitor. She needs full protection at all times now that the Cicariellos have linked her to me.

"Stop fucking fidgeting," I tell Luca. We're sitting in one of our SUVs a few blocks away while our surveillance team is in place. They'll let us know when to move in.

"I'm ready to get this shit done," he says, checking the clip in his gun for the fiftieth fucking time, driving me crazy.

"Patience—"

"Is the best way to success," he finishes for me. "Yeah, I know that stupid line father always told us. But it's not the only way to succeed."

"We're doing this right. We're not just going to kill everyone because it's easier."

"But don't you want to? This guy worked with Abrianna and betrayed her. You've killed for less."

"I know," I grit out. "And I want to. Trust me. I've thought about how I'd do it over and over, but I can't do that to her. She asked me not to hurt him."

"Doesn't mean *I* can't."

"Yes, I know. That's something I've already thought of." Luca opens his mouth to say something, but I stop him. "And no, I'm not going soft if that's what you're about to say. I'm not losing her because of my need for vengeance."

"You and Alec," he says, shaking his head.

I'm about to tell him he'll get it one day, but then the voice of one of our men comes over the intercoms in our ears, silencing us both.

"We've got movement. Two black SUVs and a blue sedan are pulling up in front of the warehouse. Sam is emerging from the passenger side of the sedan and an older man from the driver's side."

I press my finger to the small bud in my ear to unmute my com. "Send a picture of the older man right now," I demand.

Anytime we're on an op like this, we get fresh burner phones to stay linked and then wipe them clean and destroy them when we're done. When an image comes through mine and Luca's phones, I groan.

"Fuck, I had a feeling it was him."

"What the fuck?"

Another voice comes through our ears. "Two men in each SUV are getting out to greet them. Heading inside the building now."

"I've got the visual inside now." We have a man up in the rafters out of sight with a rifle. "They're approaching four crates in the rear… Opening them now… Tossing coffee bags on the ground… I've got a visual on the product, Boss. M-16's, M-4's, and ammunition in the first three. And holy fuck. Next one is holding a fucking rocket launcher and five missiles."

"You've got pictures of everything?"

"Yes, Boss. Everyone's faces and the merchandise have been captured."

"Good. Everyone move in," I command, and Alfie peels away from the curb, heading straight for the warehouse.

I have my soldiers trained in all tactical situations whether it be with weapons or hand-to-hand combat. I have a former Delta Force and SEAL on my payroll to get them in shape and know how to get in the mindset of working both solo and as a team in an organized fashion. No mistakes. Always ready for the unexpected.

It's not as if we're out on the streets starting wars, but when you have the reputation of being the best and capable of anything, you need to have the skills to back it up. No one fucks with me, my family, or my business. If they do, then they know war is coming to their doorstep.

Like right fucking now. You fuck with my woman, and I'll fuck with you right back, leaving you with nothing.

Listening to my men moving in on our targets, I hear shouts, scuffling, a few rounds popping off, and grunting as they're taken down.

Alfie pulls up to the warehouse and Luca and I hop out, shoving our guns in our shoulder holsters. We don't engage in shit these days unless we're needed.

Keeping a cool exterior while my blood rages with the need to end the lives of these sorry excuses for men, I walk through the door and straight to the back of the building.

"Well, well, well. What do we have here?" I look in the crates and then flash a sardonic smile to the four Cicariello soldiers my men have on their knees and zip tied. They fight their restraints, but each of my soldiers hits them in their backs with the barrels of their guns and they stop resisting. "I'm sure Joey isn't going to like that these are now mine." I pick up an M-14 and inspect it.

"Fuck you, Carfano." His words are dripping with disdain and I give the asshole my full attention.

"Isn't this a turn of events? You tell your daughter if she stays with me then she's dirtying her name and your family. And yet here you are, doing that all by yourself." Richard Fleming's face turns a deep red, and he puffs out a heaving breath before lunging for me. He doesn't get far on his knees, and my fist connects with his cheek before he can even attempt something. "Just so you're aware"—I smirk—"I dirtied your daughter long before you ever dared to give her that ultimatum."

"You're the one who broke Abrianna," Sam sneers. "You left her a shell of herself for me to put back together." His mouth twists up in what I can only assume is some kind of smile that's meant to be predatory, but he'll never be anything other than a frat boy trying to play tough in a world he has no business being in.

"You don't get to speak her name." I lower my voice to a chilling tone that's made men twice his size and ten times more lethal shake with fear. I step in front of him and whip my gun out, pressing the barrel to his forehead. "You know nothing about her. Or me. And you want to talk about breaking her when you're here, undermining her and everything she's built by making a deal with the scum of the earth."

Sam can play pretend all he likes, but I see the fear in his eyes. I see the tremble in his legs that threaten to give out on him.

"And you're not?" he challenges.

I press my gun harder into his skin. "That doesn't change the fact that she's mine." I take out my backup gun from my other holster and pin it to Abri's dad's forehead. "What's to stop me from ending the both of you right here and now? She's already known for a week that Sam is a lying sack of shit." His eyes flare. "She saw you last week in here with your little drug shipment."

He pales, the last bit of fire in his eyes extinguishing. "What?"

"She's known all week that you betrayed her. So any

hope you've held on to that she'd ever be yours should leave your head now." I tap the gun against the top of his head, making him flinch. "Get them to the basement," I tell the men standing behind each of them. "And the rest of you get the merchandise in the truck out back."

We've had a delivery truck waiting outside the warehouse next door, ready for extraction of the shipment and ensure safe transport to my building in Manhattan without drawing any unwanted attention.

I roll my shoulders and climb back in the SUV with Luca.

"I don't think I would've been able to hold back from either pulling the trigger or beating them to a pulp if I were you," he says.

"That's why you're not me." I watch all six men get loaded in the back of the delivery truck and shoved to the floor to be locked in to the steel rings in the sides by cuffs. "Let's go, Alfie."

I text Dante to tell him we're on our way back, but to stay with Abrianna until I get there.

After everything it has taken for us to get where we are, I'm not keeping Abri in the dark about this. She's going to get the chance to question her father and Sam alongside me.

When I walk through the door of my place, I look at Dante first. "I'll meet you downstairs," I tell him, and Abrianna jumps at the sound of my voice.

Standing, she practically runs to me. "What happened?"

First things first, I grab her around the waist and haul her against me, kissing her hard.

"There's something you should see, angel."

"Okay," she breathes, my kiss having distracted her like I

was hoping it would.

We ride the elevator down in silence, with her tucked safely at my side. Waiting for us in the basement are Luca, Nico, Gabriel, Marco, Stefano, and Dante. They're pacing the area around the grappling mats, but stop the moment I walk in.

Luca nods at me to tell me that all the men are in their cells and the product has been put in the saferoom, then he looks at Abrianna. "Hey, Abrianna."

"Hi, Luca. Everything went okay today? I mean…well, I don't know." She laughs nervously. "As well as it could go when you're stopping one of my closest friends from importing guns through my charity."

"It's why you're here, angel." I squeeze her hip and she looks up at me.

"What happened? Did something happen to Sam?" The worry in her voice makes my blood boil, but I tamp it down.

"No."

"Then what?"

"What room is he in?" I ask Luca.

"Two."

Nodding, I guide Abrianna through the gym and down the cold cement hall that has metal door after door lining the walls. I stop us at the second one. "Angel, someone else was there who's really pulling the strings. Not Sam."

Her brows pull together in confusion and then her eyes widen before she wipes her face clean of emotion. "Open the door, Leo," she tells me, her voice strong and unwavering.

When I do as she says, Abrianna storms inside and steps right up to her father.

He's sitting in a metal chair, hands cuffed behind his

back and ankles secured to the legs of the chair.

"You knew?" she accuses, not wasting any time.

"Abri, honey, tell him to let me go," her father says in mock exasperation, as if this is all just some misunderstanding and mild inconvenience for him.

"No," my girl fires back. "And don't call me 'honey.' You no longer want to be associated with me. Or did you forget already?"

Richard's face morphs, dropping his innocent act. "Whatever you think you know, you have no idea, little girl."

"I already found out what Sam has been doing. For how long, I don't know, but we can clear up anything else I don't know right now, starting with you telling me what your roll is in all of this."

Her father barks out an evil laugh and my jaw clenches. "You're so naïve."

I want to fuck him up so badly right now, but this is Abri's time. She needs this. She needs to learn for herself who her father is and decide what we'll do with him.

Her hands fist at her sides and she says through a clenched jaw, "Then why don't you enlighten me?"

"You think I let you and your mother start your charities out of the goodness of my heart?" His eyes darken. "With my fucking money I worked years and countless hours for?"

I'm standing behind Abri, silently giving her my support, but not interfering. Her father is a piece of shit millionaire, twenty times over, who made his money by being a ruthless businessman. He's not one to share what's his unless he can profit from it.

"Yes, that's what I thought. You've been using the charity in L.A. to smuggle in drugs and guns too?"

"Now you're catching on," he says condescendingly.

"And when I wanted to start one here?" she probes, the worry in her voice making me want to shield her from what her father is going to say. He's going to break her heart and she knows it.

"I have a friend here in the city who put me in contact with the right people."

"Does mom know?"

He barks out a harsh laugh. "God, no. I promised myself to keep you both in the dark. Sam and I had it all worked out."

Abri shakes her head and takes a step back. "You roped Sam into all of this and you still thought he and I should be together?"

My fists clench at my sides.

"Honey, he wanted to be roped in. I laid it all out for him before he came to New York to work with you, and he jumped at the chance to make more money."

"Stop." The command leaves Abri with such force, her father looks up at her with surprise in his eyes. "You've been lying to me for almost a decade now. You're not the man I've called my father my entire life. You had the nerve to demand I choose between you and Leo because you're somehow the better choice?" Her voice goes up at the end in anger. "You're a liar and a cheat."

"And he isn't?" Richard spits out, nodding his chin towards me.

"Whatever and whoever Leo is, he admits to it and lives it out in the open. He's never pretended to be anyone other than who he is. Especially to me. *We're done, dad,*" she growls, the little demon in her coming out. "And everything you've done to ruin any good mom and I have accomplished is done, too." Spinning around, Abrianna walks past me and straight out the door.

CHAPTER 28
Abrianna

Striding out of the cell's door, I walk a few paces down the hall, my chest heaving with labored breaths. The fact that my father is in a cement cell in the basement of Leo's building is making my head spin.

The heavy metal door slams closed and I turn and walk back to Leo. "I thought I was doing good work. I thought I was making a difference. I thought my dad was a good man. I thought Sam was my friend. I thought I–"

"Shh, baby. Come here." Leo cuts off my rant by pulling me in and wrapping his arms around me, giving me some of his strength.

"Leo." I choke on his name, clutching the lapels of his

suit while I bury my face in his chest.

With him surrounding me in his strength, I let all the emotions threating to destroy me, out. When he feels me trembling as angry tears spill from my eyes, his arms around me tighten.

"Don't cry, angel. He's not worth it."

"I'm not crying over him," I assure Leo, craning my neck back to look up at him. I blink my tears away. "I'm crying because I'm mad. Sometimes that's the only way to get it out of me. I'm mad that I didn't know, and mad that I was used as a pawn and front in some game my dad and Sam had to make more money. Why is it always about money?"

"What do you want to do, angel? Just say the word and I'll take care of this for you."

"I don't want you to kill him. I just want this to be over." Whatever that ends up looking like. "But I need to talk to Sam first. Where is he?"

"In the next room probably."

I swipe my face clear of tears and take a few deep breaths. "Alright." Leo places his hand on my lower back and walks me over to the next metal door.

I nod to him and he opens it, showing me Sam secured to a metal chair in the middle of the room just like my dad. His head is hanging low, looking defeated and tired, but he snaps it up at the sound of us entering.

"Abri," he breathes, as if he's relieved to see me. "You're here."

I tilt my head to the side. "Of course I am."

"Abri, I'm so sorry."

"At least you have the decency to sound sincere."

"I am."

"Sam, you and my father have been lying to me for the past five years. And my father, longer. But you, Sam, I thought you were my friend. I thought you cared about me. You told me you loved me."

"I do," he says, his eyes pleading with me.

"Save it. My father let me take you with me because he needed someone he trusted handling the books so your little operation went unnoticed by me and everyone else." I shake my head in disgust. "I must seem like such an idiot to you."

"No, Abri, no. I hated lying to you. But your dad wanted to always keep your mom and you in the dark in case something ever went south."

"I don't think you're understanding how much you betrayed me. The City's Angels was my everything when I had nothing." My voice catches, and I feel Leo shift behind me. "You were what I had when I had nothing, Sam." A tear slips down my cheek. "And it was all just some front for thugs to move guns, drugs, and God only knows what else. The money I used to help people with was dirty and came at the price of putting weapons on the streets and poison in people's blood. How many lives do you think I'm responsible for ending because I asked my father for help?" More unwanted tears escape down my cheeks.

"Don't think like that, Abri."

"Don't tell me how to think," I growl out, my anger coming to a boil. "No one has the right to try and tell me how to think or feel right now." Spinning around, I walk straight to Leo, who's let me have my space to figure this all out. I grab the back of his neck and pull him down for a kiss.

Right now, I feel like kissing the man who has broken me in ways I'll never fully heal from, but has also mended me in a way only he knew how to and was capable of.

Leo kisses me back with a hunger I never want to cease. I always want him hungry for me.

Gripping his suit's lapels in my fists, I pull back just enough to look him in the eyes. "Thank you for this, Leo. And I know what this will all mean as a fallout for my family, but–"

"Come on, angel," he says low. "We'll talk options."

Turning towards Sam, I walk right up to him. "Whatever part of you thought I would ever love you after knowing that you destroyed everything, is insane."

"You were never supposed to find out," he says, and the next thing I know, my palm is burning from slapping him across the face.

"I never want to see you again," I grit out, turning on my heel. I walk out of that room and down the hall back to the gym area where Leo's family is waiting.

All eyes turn to me as I heave in breath after breath, trying to get my lungs to work without collapsing from the pressure.

"She okay?" I hear one of them ask.

"I'm fine," I bite back, directing it at no one in particular. "What are my options?" I ask Leo, stopping my pacing to stare up at him, my eyes pleading for him to give me a solution to a problem I never imagined facing.

"Options?" one of the men scoffs, but I don't turn my head to see who said it. I keep my eyes on Leo.

"Shut the fuck up," Leo growls. "She gets to choose what happens to them."

I can't help the little smile that tugs at my lips. He's sexy when he's bossy. "First choice – we do nothing. I seized all their shit from this deal, which is enough for the Cicariellos to cut ties with your business."

"But my father helps someone else in L.A."

"Yes. But the Cicariellos will most likely kill your father and Sam for screwing everything up."

I swallow hard. "Second option?"

"One I have never done. But I can send everything I have on the both of them to the FBI and let them take care of it."

My eyes widen. "Wouldn't that just come back on you?" I don't want Leo getting indicted for anything by involving the feds.

"No, baby." He smirks. "I have a guy who'd take the evidence without question and make sure my name stayed out of it."

"But then they'd go to prison," I say more to myself than anyone in the room.

"Yes."

"And I would, too. Why would they believe that I knew nothing about it?"

"I'd never let that happen," he assures me.

"Is there a third option?"

"Not one I want to offer." Leo grips the side of my neck in a caress. "Anyone else gets a bullet between the eyes after they're worked over so good, they're practically begging for death. But for you, angel, I'll let you decide their fate."

"Thank you," I breathe, closing my eyes briefly. I can feel the eyes of the men in the room on us, but I still whisper, "I love you."

Leo's eyes turn to liquid black — molten pools of contained emotion he doesn't show outwardly. But I see it. I feel it.

"What do you want to do?"

"I hate them right now, but I don't want them dead. I can't be the reason for that."

I know being with Leo will always have its battles, I just didn't think one of them would be tearing apart my own family and ruining a ten-year friendship.

"You don't have to decide right now, angel. Let me figure something out for you. I'll take care of it."

"I trust you," I whisper, and his eyes flare.

CHAPTER 29
Leo

Abrianna is an amazing fucking woman, and she's mine. When I told her I'd take care of it for her, she looked at me with such trust. Like I'm everything she needs.

My family counts on me and knows I'll always do what's needed to protect us and ensure our success on every level. It's my job. But with Abrianna, it's more than a job. It's my purpose.

She doesn't want anything from me other than me. And the fact that she doesn't want me to give her the world, makes me want to give it to her all the more.

"What are we going to do with the others?" Luca asks when I come back down from bringing Abri back up to my place.

"We're going to make them talk." I may have let Abri decide what happens to her dad and Sam, but the Cicariello soldiers are mine to do with what I want.

Luca flashes me an evil grin. "Let's get started."

Taking my suit jacket off, I drape it on a chair in the gym and roll the sleeves of my white dress shirt up. My father used to make me do all the 'talking' when he was still around. He wanted to ensure I would be like him. And in a way I am, even when I want to think otherwise while I'm with Abri.

I am my father's son. I'm cut from the same cloth. His blood runs through my veins.

And it's in these moments that I'm thankful to him for making me the man I am. I may have hated him, but I always respected him. It was a battle I waged every day when he was alive. But despite however I felt in the moment, no one gets away with murdering him or my uncle. And no one gets to think they can take everything my family has built over decades of hard work.

The fucking arrogance.

The moment I took over, I showed them just how wrong they were, and to never try that shit with me or my family again.

I came at them hard. So hard, I sent them running into hiding, and I've been waiting for this moment to finally eliminate them.

Joey, their boss, is first.

"Leo." I turn to see Alec and Vinny walking through the door, looks of pure determination on their faces. I called them right after we left the warehouse, and they drove straight up here. I would never keep either of them away from this.

"I brought Tessa up to your place," Alec tells me. "I wasn't leaving her alone, and I thought your girl could use the company."

I nod. "She could."

"How is she?" Vinny asks.

"She'll be fine." My girl is strong.

"Let's get started." Alec rubs his hands together and stretches his neck from side to side like he's getting ready for battle.

"Dante," I call. "Bring them out here."

One by one, Dante brings out the four men, pushing them to their knees on the cement in front of the grappling mats, on display before all of us.

The one in the middle was the one calling the shots this morning, and Dante steps up behind him, gripping his hair and pulling his head back. The other three men lift their heads on their own. They thought they were acting tough this morning, but now they look like they're going to piss themselves.

"How's Joey?" I ask the one in Dante's grip, tilting my head to the side.

"He'll be great once you're dead," he fires back like a rabid animal.

I step towards him, looking down at him with a satisfied sneer. "Well, isn't that a coincidence, because I feel the same way about him. And you're going to tell me everything he's been planning."

His eyes flare with a crazed gleam. I know this asshole has every intention of resisting me, but he'll soon learn that resisting is futile. They always break in the end. It's just a matter of how long and how much they're willing to endure before that happens.

When we threw them in the cells, Stefano took their wallets, and he hands me them now.

"Who do the Cicariellos smuggle the drugs and guns for?" I look down at the IDs. "Nick?" He struggles against his restraints, but doesn't answer.

I give Dante a small nod and he punches Nick in the kidney, eliciting a deep grunt and gasp for air.

"Who do the Cicariellos smuggle the drugs and guns for?" I ask again. And again, when he doesn't answer, I give the nod for another punch to the kidney. The look of pure agony on his face is enough to fill me with excitement. Testing a man's threshold for pain is an art, and it's been a while since I've gotten to witness it for myself.

"It only gets worse from here unless you talk. How much loyalty could you possibly have for a family who operates from behind the walls of a compound like pussies?" I step up to him and bend so he sees the inevitable in my eyes. "I made that happen. And I assure you, whatever they've told you about me and my family, the reality is worse."

I straighten and look at the other three IDs in my hand and look between the men. "Alessio, Andre, and Franco. Do any of you want to tell me what I want to know? Or do you need persuading?"

The one on the left, Andre, looks like he wants to talk, but he presses his lips together to keep from doing so. He knows if he caves with just a threat it will make him a dead man with his boss. If he even leaves this basement before I do the honors myself.

"Alec? Luca? Nico?" I offer the men up like a gift to my brothers and cousin, and they step up to their choice.

The sound of fists colliding with the faces of the men and their cheek bones crunching under the pressure has me slipping further into the dark murky water that always threatens to pull me under entirely. It used to be Abrianna's light I'd cling to when I knew I was going too far, but now she's the reason I'm going deeper instead.

Alec grips Alessio's throat and as his face turns red from lack of oxygen. We all went through the same training, but each of us took it differently and changed us in different ways.

Uncle Sal was my father's underboss, just as Luca is mine, and at times we hated them.

At times we wished we were anyone but who we were.

But we never gave in to our weakest moments or thoughts. We've seen each other at our worst, but made sure it never lasted.

Michael Carfano may have been a bastard in his own right, but I knew what he was doing. He made all of my cousins and brothers and I forge bonds with one another that nothing could break. I know as well as the rest of them that we'd all die before we gave anything up to an enemy.

We're connected by more than just blood.

I was the first to turn ten, which meant for a long time, I was the sole focus of my father's attention. I lied to my brother's and told them I was always sore and bruised from taking karate classes. I knew they were suspicious about the sudden change in me and my relationship with our father, but they somehow knew not to ask.

I went through hell and came out a man others fear just

by my name alone. And I fucking revel in that. I live for it. It's what makes me know-now that I am, and can be, man enough for Abrianna, and be able to protect her. Always.

Despite being put through the ringer longer and harder than anyone else, it doesn't diminish the strength, abilities, and darkness that lives within all of us. We're all capable of more than our calm exteriors and five-thousand-dollar custom suits might convey.

"Tell us who you're smuggling for," Alec growls, releasing Alessio's throat before he passes out. He sucks in ragged breaths.

"How about you?" Luca prompts, punching Andre in the jaw, the family ring on his finger slicing his skin open. "You want to talk?"

Andre groans and flexes his jaw, and Luca goes in for another punch. "This won't stop until you talk. It's your choice if you want to get beaten to the brink of death before that happens or not. I personally like that option."

Nico goes for the gut punch and then an uppercut to the jaw, making Franco's head snap back.

I remain silent, and when no one talks, I give Dante a small nod and he pulls his knife out, holding it under the chin of his guy. He's always been partial to knives when it comes to his work. "Have you ever passed out from pain?" he asks in a chilling tone. He knows where to cut to keep a man alive for an extended period of time while bringing him to his limit with blood loss. "Talk and you can still say that you haven't. No?" Placing the tip of the knife behind his ear, Dante cuts into his skin on both sides, making Nick grunt out in pain.

He keeps his lips sealed, so Dante gets to work on him while Alec, Luca, and Nico work the other three over in a more primitive way.

Eventually, they break. They always do.

"Okay," Nick croaks. His voice is broken and raw, and his face is covered in rivers of blood, making it hard to see his mouth move. "I'll talk."

"Good. We'll start with who you're smuggling for."

"The Latin Kings."

Fuck. They're the biggest gang in the city, and while none of our business dealings cross paths, I don't want to go to war with them. But once they find out their pipeline into the city is no longer viable, they're going to want to retaliate.

I'm going to have to either give them another option or let them keep using the charity.

"When do they expect delivery for the guns?"

"Tomorrow night at eight in one of their stash houses in the Bronx."

"Luca," I bark, and we walk a few feet away. "This is more complicated than I thought."

"We don't need to get tangled up in gang shit."

"I know." Striding back up to Nick, Dante pulls his head back, his eyes now defeated. "What do you think your boss is willing to do for his shipment back?"

"Dom and Geno are running things now, and they need this deal to go through."

"What about Joey and Tino?"

"They think they're in charge but they haven't been for a while. Too fucked up."

"Fucked up?"

"Yeah. Paranoid and shit. Dom and Geno do all the work now."

"Phone password," I demand, and Nick's eyes shift to

the side before meeting mine again. "Now."

Blood drips from his mouth as he says, "2-2-4-1."

Stefano has their phones on a table and hooked up to his laptop so he can copy all the information on them.

"Which one is his?"

"You know I trust you, Leo, but what's the plan here?"

"We're going to make a deal."

"What?"

"You heard me. Now, which one is his phone?"

Stefano knows not to question me again, and so he silently hands me one of the phones. I put in the passcode and find a string of unread messages sent from a blocked number I can only assume is Dom or Geno. I press call and hold the phone to my ear.

"Where the fuck are you, Nicky? You were supposed to be here hours ago. What went wrong?" Just the sound of his voice makes my blood boil.

"What went wrong is that you thought I wouldn't find out."

There's a long pause on the other end before he growls, "Carfano."

"That's right. And if you want your shipment, then you're going to meet me to talk."

"Where?"

"Be at the warehouse in an hour. Just you and your brother. I'll have a car waiting."

"Fine," he clips.

"And if you even think of trying anything, you'll be dead on the spot."

"Fine," he says again, hanging up.

"Bring them back to their cells. Then I want Alfie and

Dante in one car, and Gabriel and Marco in another. Get a team surrounding the warehouse in the next half hour and bring them back here." I bark out orders and everyone gets moving.

CHAPTER 30
Abrianna

"How are you holding up?" Tessa asks me when I walk into the living room. Alec dropped her off here before meeting Leo down in the basement, and she insisted I take a long hot bath to relax before we talked.

"Fine," I tell her.

"I'm one of the few people who will understand what you're feeling. Trust me. I know what being with a Carfano man means."

She's right, and I find myself blurting out what's been on my mind. "Every man I've ever loved has lied to me and betrayed me at some point. My father, Sam, Leo. They've all hurt me."

"Well, you found a way to forgive Leo, right?"

"That's different. He's different. Leo and I…" I trail off, not sure how to put into words how we're different.

She smiles softly. "I know what you mean. Alec really hurt me, too. And I honestly didn't want to forgive him. But there was no way I was going to live without him."

"I know that feeling well."

"They're obsessed with safety precautions, but that doesn't deter from the fact that all of the men downstairs will protect you with everything they have."

I tuck my feet up on the couch. "I know. I just don't want them to have to do that. I don't want anyone getting hurt because of me."

"This is more than just you now, though. Once they found out who was behind it all, there was no way they weren't going to do anything."

"I know." What the Cicariellos did was the beginning of the end for Leo and I. I can't help but think that if they hadn't been behind Leo's dad and uncle's murders then we might have been together longer. It was Leo stepping into his father's shoes that had him realizing he couldn't have the both of us.

"How did you and Alec meet?" I ask her to distract myself.

She smiles. "I dance in his casino's Friday night show, and he came to watch me every week. He sat at the same table and always left me flowers and gifts at my dressing station for me to find after the show."

"Really? That's so sweet."

She laughs. "Don't let Alec hear you say that. I don't think anyone's ever described him as sweet."

I laugh too. "True. Leo either." Even though I've seen his moments, I know no one else has.

"And just a testament to how crazy these men are about safety, Alec had someone following me for weeks and I had no idea."

My eyes widen. "What?"

"Yeah," she says with a laugh, then sobers like a sad memory just came to mind. "I was mad about it, but grateful on the night I needed him. It was the night I officially met Alec, actually. And I won't say it's been easy, but I would do anything for him, and vice versa. That man is…" She shakes her head. "He's everything."

That about sums up how I would describe Leo, too.

"But enough about them." She smiles. "How about I order us some food and we can open a bottle of something expensive and watch a movie?"

"Sounds like the perfect plan."

* * * *

I'm glad Tessa is here. For the past couple of hours, we've devoured Chinese food and watched a movie. If I were alone, I'd be going crazy wondering what was happening down in the basement.

When the credits start to roll, I down the rest of the wine in my glass. "Do you want to watch another?" she asks.

"Yeah. You pick. I'm going to go get us more wine."

"I was just thinking that." She smiles.

We watch another movie and start a third, but I'm so tired, I fall asleep ten minutes into it.

I only wake up when I'm lifted from the couch and

carried down the hall.

"Leo? Are you okay?" I ask, half asleep.

"Yeah, angel. Just sleep. We'll talk in the morning."

"Okay," I whisper, tucking my face into his chest.

CHAPTER 31
Leo

I'm pacing in the basement, waiting for Alfie, Dante, and the others to bring Dom and Geno back here. I need to make sure I keep myself in check or I know shit will get out of control. I can't let my anger and hatred cloud my judgement. I don't have that luxury.

My phone vibrates in my pocket and I pull it out to see a message from Gabriel telling me they have them and are on their way back now.

I want to have full control over the situation, but I don't want them to see how we operate, so I had Dante make sure they were hooded before putting them in the car.

When they arrive, they're walked through the gym and

down past the shooting range to the meeting room we have down here.

We usually use the conference room on one of the floors above us when we have meetings like this, but this room is more secluded and suitable for today. I don't want those fuckers to be comfortable. I want them to be looking at four walls and me – the one who holds their fate.

Dante and Gabriel push them down into chairs and then rip their hoods off. The brothers blink and dart their eyes around, taking in everything and everyone.

"So, this is your place?" Dom asks like a cocky little asshole, reaching up to fix his hair. "Not what I pictured the great and powerful Leo Carfano to use as his office," he says, his words dripping with sarcasm. The fucking prick.

"Let's cut the shit, Dom."

"Fine by me," he says, dropping the act. "We want our shipment. I know you don't want the Latin Kings finding out that it was taken by you or that it was your girl's foundation we've been using as transport."

My vision blurs, blinding me with rage.

"I see your anger already. So, we're prepared to make a deal with you."

"What kind of deal?" I grit out.

"One where we all get what we want," Geno says.

"And you know what I want?"

"Our father," Dom says simply.

I feel everyone around me looking at one another, but my eyes are glued to Dom's, reading the truth in them.

"You're willing to give us your father for the weapons?" Nothing is that simple.

"We want a little bit more than that." When I don't

answer, he continues. "We're done working and living in hiding because of what our father did. He made that decision five years ago on his own. We had nothing to do with it, and neither did our uncles. He obviously wasn't thinking clearly, and we've been paying for it ever since."

"Are you getting to the point?"

"We don't want you trying to kill us when we leave our compound. Our father is fucking crazy and I'm tired of dealing with him and his paranoia."

"You're willing to trade your father for the ability to leave your house?"

"It's been five fucking years. Yes, we are. We've been running things for a while now, and we want him out of the way. You do that, and we'll make sure your girl's name is never mentioned to the Latin Kings. Of course we'll need a new connection to receive shipments, since I'm sure you've already killed them." The balls on these two. They're referring to Abri's dad and Sam.

"We haven't."

Their eyes widen. "Huh. Interesting."

"A few days of sitting in a cement box can do wonders for a man's state of mind. They tend to be a lot more accommodating the next time they see you," I say as a cover.

"Whatever you say. Now, do we have a deal?"

"I can get you another warehouse to move your product."

"No. We need the business attached to it to be legitimate. Not just some empty warehouse we're shipping coffee to."

"I know," I grind out, infuriated at their insinuation that I don't fucking know that. "I have a coffee shop to link it to that you can have." I bought my mother's favorite coffee shop years ago when it was struggling, but she rarely goes into the city anymore, and wouldn't even know if I took her gift back.

I'm showing more cards in my deck than I ever do, but this is for Abrianna. If this doesn't work, then I'm going to have to go back to her and tell her that I have to let her father and Sam go back to doing what they were doing. Otherwise, she'd be at risk. And I'm not fucking letting anything happen to her because of her family. Her father never thought of her or her mother when he wanted to make his pockets deeper.

Some men let the poison of money and power control them. They're weak.

The brothers sit in silence for a moment before Dom speaks. "You want to give us one of your legitimate businesses and a warehouse," he says as a statement, not understanding my motives.

"For your father. And to never use the Fleming Family Foundation for any of your shipments again. I'll know if you do," I tell him. "Then this little truce we're building will be voided and I'll make sure none of you live to see another day."

"She must have a golden pussy," Geno scoffs, and Dom pins him with a look as the men around the room all take a step towards them.

"Shut the fuck up," Dom grinds out to his younger brother, then meets my narrowed eyes. He swallows. "I apologize for him."

I could so easily just kill these scumbags, but I need something only they can give me. So after a beat, I raise my chin in acceptance.

"We don't want our father or other members in our family finding out about this," Dom continues. "We'll give you the codes to the security system, a floor plan of the compound, and tell you where he'll be on that day and at what time."

"It sounds like you've been planning this for longer than the car ride over here."

"We have. It's time. We were going to contract it out to make it look like you ordered it, but this is so much simpler."

This is fucking great. They think they were going to pin their own hit on their father to me? I never would have claimed it. And believe me, I want every family to know when I get my revenge.

"Yes, it is. Because that never would've worked and I would have killed you for taking that opportunity away from me. Besides, I have better plans for your father that you wouldn't be able to stomach."

"We don't care what you do."

A few of the men around the room choke out dark laughs under their breaths.

"Alright, then."

With a map of their compound drawn out and a date and time set, all I need is Abri waiting naked and wet for me, and I'll be fucking set.

"Do you think there's a chance this is a setup?" Alec asks me in the elevator ride up to my penthouse.

"There's always a chance, but I don't think so this time. They really want out of their current situation."

"Some fucking loyalty they have," he admonishes.

"I knew they'd break eventually."

"You knew this would happen?"

"Not exactly. I just knew I'd drive them to do something that would make them come to me."

Alec shakes his head. "I forget how fucking crazy you are. You're always two steps ahead of the rest of us, but you never show it, or let us in on it."

I slap him on the back as the elevator doors slide open. "I am crazy. I just hide it better than most."

Alec surprises me with a small smile and shake of his head. Jesus fucking Christ, Tessa is a miracle worker. I haven't seen Alec smile in as long as it's been since I have.

We walk into the living room to find both of our girls fast asleep on opposite ends of the couch.

"*Bella*," Alec murmurs, tucking Tessa's hair behind her ear. She stirs, blinking up at him with a dreamy little smile. It's the same way my angel looks at me, so I know Alec knows exactly how it feels to have something so precious in his life that he would do anything to make sure he saw that look every fucking day until he dies.

Helping Tessa to her feet, Alec puts his arm around her to keep her steady. "We're going to stay in my place downstairs since it's late. Text if you're having another meeting in the morning, otherwise I'll just head back to AC and come back on Saturday."

I nod and he leaves. Below my penthouse suite that covers the entirety of the top floor of my building, is Luca's place, which also occupies the entire floor. Then below that are ten floors of apartments for family and guests when I need them all close by. My uncles all have houses out in

Jersey or Staten Island now that they don't have an extensively active role in the day-to-day operations of our business dealings, but my cousins all live here.

Abrianna looks at peace for the first time since she found all of this shit out. So instead of waking her, I lift her into my arms and carry her to our bed.

"Leo? Are you okay?" she croaks in her sexy sleep-filled voice, stirring in my arms.

"Yeah, angel. We'll talk in the morning. Just sleep."

"Okay," she whispers, tucking herself against me with implicit trust. She'll never know what it does to me. There aren't words to describe it.

Pulling the sheets back, I lay her down on her side of the bed. After a quick shower to rid me of everything that happened today, I slide in beside her and pull her against me. She sighs in her sleep and wraps her arm around me while tucking her face against my chest.

I breathe a sigh of relief knowing she'll be okay. I left all those years ago to protect her, but knowing I'm the only one who can protect her now gives me new life. She gives me renewed purpose. I always knew what that was since I was a boy, but she's changed that again.

She's changed everything for me. And I don't want to go back. Ever. Every risk is worth it, and I know she'll fight just as hard as I will through any and everything that will be thrown at us.

CHAPTER 32
Abrianna

Fingers running up and down my spine lull me awake, and I tighten my hold on the warm body next to me.

I plant a kiss to the smooth skin closest to me and Leo groans softly, so I do it again, this time letting my tongue peek out for a taste.

"Mmm," I hum. He tastes like his body wash – spicy oranges. I lick him again out of pure need to have his taste forever imprinted in my memory, but Leo growls, rolling on top of me and pining my hands above my head in a swift move that makes my head spin.

"You need a taste, angel?"

"Yes," I breathe, the look in his eyes making my skin

crackle with heat. I arch into him, wanting him closer, and wanting him all over me, all at once. I don't want to feel anything but him. "I need you to take it all away," I whisper, and his eyes darken. "I just need you right now."

Leaning down, Leo presses a kiss to my eager lips. "I'm going to take your pain, angel. I'll always take your pain and wear it as my own."

Tears sting my eyes, but they don't have the chance to form because Leo kisses me deep into the pillows. Licking the seam of my lips, I open for him and he sweeps inside of my mouth, his hot tongue sliding against mine in a dance we know as well as breathing.

The pain I've felt in my chest is pulled from me like a spirit leaving my body, finding a new home inside of Leo. He takes my every thought and replaces them with memories of him and I that show me they're not just our past, but our future as well.

He's giving me my future in this kiss.

He's giving me everything I've ever wanted. Him.

Keeping my hands together above my head with one of his, Leo kisses his way down my neck, my chest heaving under his mouth while I suck in ragged breaths as if I've just run a marathon. My lungs are on fire. I'm on fire. And from his kiss alone, he gives me this.

Pulling down the neck of my tank top and bra, Leo swirls his skilled tongue around my nipple and sucks it deep into his mouth, making my hips buck against his. I feel his hard length through his boxers and I moan into the quiet of the morning.

He repeats the same beautiful torture to my other nipple, and I cry out at the lightning strike that spikes through me at his hard pull, as if he's physically taking my pain from me.

"Leo," I choke out, and he bites down on my breast before continuing down my torso. Bunching my shirt up to my breasts, he plants open mouthed kisses everywhere he can reach.

My breathy sighs turn to moans as he releases my hands and peels my leggings and panties from my body. The cool morning air makes my skin pebble with goosebumps, but quickly turns to fire under his touch.

Parting my legs, Leo doesn't hesitate or ease into anything. He makes a long pass with his tongue through my folds, groaning at how slick I am for him. I cry out at the contact, every nerve ending in my body on high alert, sensitive to everything he does.

"I can't wait, angel. I need you too badly," he rasps, leaving me for an instant to strip from his boxers.

"Please," I plea, needing him inside of me more than anything.

Hovering above me, Leo hesitates, his eyes boring into mine with an intensity that would scare me if I didn't already know he would never hurt me.

"Abri, I..." he trails off, lowering his forehead to mine for a moment before pulling back to show me what he can't say.

I cup his face with both of my hands, stroking his cheeks. "I love you, Leo." His dark eyes flare with heat. "And I know you love me, too." His eyes flare again.

"You seem to know everything, angel," he says roughly, his deep voice full of devotion and love.

"Not everything. But I know at least one more thing."
"What's that?"

"You're going to fuck me hard and fast, and then long and slow."

Growling, Leo kisses me hard, hooking his hands behind my knees and pulling my legs up and open, entering me fully in a single thrust. My throat closes around a scream from the swift intrusion, but it's good. So good. Leo simultaneously stretches me wide while hitting a place deep inside of me only he can reach.

"You have it wrong, angel," Leo tells me, holding himself right there inside of me while licking the column of my neck to rasp in my ear, "I'm going to go torturously slow until you're creaming all over me, and then I'm going to fuck you so hard you won't be able to walk."

"Yes," I sigh, spreading my legs wider.

Leo bites down on my earlobe and pulls out of me slowly, letting me feel every inch of him before pushing back inside of me.

Fuuucckkk.

How he's even able to fit is a miracle.

I shudder with the feeling of complete fullness taking over. I'm full of him in the most intimate of ways – our bodies connected like two missing puzzle pieces finally finding their place.

My heart is so full of the love I have for him and the love he has for me. A love that is unlike anything anyone else will ever know or understand, which makes it all the more filling – body, heart, and soul.

True to his word, Leo keeps up the torturously slow pace until my body is quivering and shaking beneath him. The buildup reaches its climax as my inner walls flutter and then squeeze and convulse around him.

I rake my nails across the width of his back as Leo continues to push in and out of me, letting me ride the waves flowing through me before gripping my hips and flipping me onto my stomach. Slapping my ass, he lifts my hips in the air and spreads my ass cheeks apart with his tight grip. The cool air on my wet center has me moaning into the pillows before he quickly reenters me, hard and fast, easily sliding through my slickness.

I scream out at the new position and the feeling of him filling my already sensitive core. But Leo has a promise to make good on, and he's never disappointed me before.

Pulling almost all the way out, he slams back in. Over and over, Leo takes me at a relentless pace that has me bracing myself on the edge of the mattress where it meets the headboard with every ounce of strength I have.

The feral sounds coming from him are driving me crazy, and the pressure in me building for the second time is sure to surpass the first with its intensity.

Leo lifts my hips to a higher angle, and that's all it takes for me to explode. Screaming my throat raw into the pillow, black dots swim in my vison as I'm dragged into the abyss. As if I've shattered into a million little pieces, Leo's grip on my hips is the only thing keeping me from completely falling apart.

His own roar fills my ears and I feel his hot come fill me with such force, I can practically taste it on my tongue.

I milk him for every drop he has, and after what feels like hours, I'm able to swim to the surface and take my first real breath in what feels like just as long.

My arms collapse from their grip and I fall to the bed. Leo pulls out of me and I feel our combined juices spill out.

Swiping his finger through it, he turns me over and holds his finger to my lips. "Taste us, angel," he demands, and I don't hesitate in licking his finger clean.

"Mmm," I hum, and his eyes darken at my approval. We taste like life. Like love. Like power.

I rub my thighs together, wanting to keep us there. I want him to paint me in our love, and I think he can read it in my eyes, because he slips two fingers between my thighs and drags them up and around my belly button.

"I want to see this swollen with my baby," he tells me, and my eyes widen, tears gathering immediately.

"You do?"

"Yes." He nods, leaning forward to lick our come from my skin in the same path he drew. "You'll be the best mother. I want to see that. You'll give them the balance they need with me as their father."

Sliding my fingers through his hair, I smile down at him. "Leo, you'll be an incredible father. I have absolute faith in you."

"That's because God himself made you for me. An angel to keep one of his fallen soldiers from becoming what he fears the most."

"What's that?" I whisper, afraid to know.

"The devil himself."

"Leo." My voice breaks on his name, and I pull him up to me so he's laying fully on top of me. "You may do bad things, but you're not a bad man. You'll never be the devil. Not to me."

Closing his eyes, Leo leans his forehead against mine, and we lay like this – lips just a breath away, breathing each other in.

"I love you, angel."

"I love you too," I whisper back, pressing my lips to his in a kiss where I give him everything I have in my heart, hoping he can feel it.

CHAPTER 33
Leo

Alec came back to the city last night, which means Tessa and Abrianna are under guard by four of our men in case this whole fucking thing turns out to be a setup or goes horribly wrong.

We've spent the week planning out every detail of the raid with contingencies for everything we could think of. But there's always the possibility for something we have no control over. Like if Dom and Geno didn't tell us everything we need to know, or if the security codes have changed.

If that happens though, we'll just light the whole fucking place up until all that's left of them and their compound is a pile of rubble and ash.

The Boss

We've kept their guns, rocket launcher, and missiles until we have Joey in our possession. Then there's a truck waiting to pass them off at a nearby secluded spot. But if something goes wrong, I can have that rocket launcher in my hands and lighting the night sky up like the fourth of fucking July.

Alfie is driving the SUV carrying Luca, Alec, and I, with Vinny and Nico in the one behind us, and two in front of us filled with five men each.

Stefano is our resident hacker, and is staying in a car right outside of the compound to disable their security system and anything else that might stand in our way. Gabriel and Marco are with the truck in a nearby abandoned lot with five of our soldiers ready for the exchange when they get the word.

We had to let Dom and Geno go last week even though every part of me wanted to throw them in a hole and call it a day. But I needed them to go back in order to make this all look legitimate and to not raise any suspicions that would make Joey's paranoia spike, causing him to go into hiding.

We have linked intercoms in our ears, but for the entire drive, we've been silent. We all have a job to do, and they know I need them focused and going over everything in their heads right now.

The brick walls surrounding the Cicariello compound rise tall from the grass as if they were guarding people worthy of the protection. As we approach the iron gates, Alfie slows, and I speak to Stefano through the com.

"Approaching now. You ready Stef?"

"Yeah." I hear his fingers flying over the keyboard that's in front of him. "Security cameras have been cut and anyone checking will see a continuous loop of nothing."

"Good."

"I've overridden their control of the gate, and it should be opening in 3, 2, 1…"

"Car 1, go," I instruct, and as all four SUVs clear the gate and tear down the driveway, my blood rushes with adrenalin. "Let's fucking do this. You know your jobs, everyone."

I get an array of hollers in agreement and I pull my guns from their holsters to triple check that they're loaded, with Luca and Alec following suit.

I take a deep breath and roll my shoulders back.

Our SUVs come to a stop outside of the Cicariello's gaudy mansion, but the three of us wait until the two teams of five have taken their places outside the front door before we climb out and take our place with Vinny and Nico.

Dante holds his hand up in a fist and then waves the two men beside him forward. The doors were left open for us, and we slip in quietly, none of us making a sound besides the soft impact of our boots on the marble floor.

On Sundays, Dom told us the family has a big dinner while the guards are all together in their house that's about an acre away from the main house in the backyard. It's the best night to do this since after the family dinner, Joey has his weekly private massage in his room and will be unprotected.

In two-man formation, we walk up the marbled staircase and bear left, making our way through the massive house along the route we planned out from the blueprint floor plans given to us.

The rooms we pass with open doors have the furniture covered in white cloths as if they're never used or bothered to be kept up with since they have no one to entertain or visit.

I've made an exception and have chosen to come on this mission with my men. This is personal. Which is why Alec, Luca, Nico, and Vinny are all here too. I would've normally left it to Gabriel, Marco, and Stefano to handle with their teams, but there was no way we were all sitting back on this. We've waited too long for this. And to be honest, I want to see the look on the bastard's face when I walk in.

We have a driver waiting in every SUV, ready to get us out of here, and we left two men at the front door in case any of the guards or family members wander into the foyer.

"Approaching the bedroom door now."

"No movement in the rest of the house," Stefano says back, monitoring the security feeds.

Dante goes in first with four men flooding in right behind. I hear the masseuse scream and Joey yelling, "Who the fuck are you? How did you get in here?"

No one answers him, and a path is made for me as I step into the room. "Good to see you again, Joey. It's been a while."

"How the fuck did you get in here, Leo?" he growls, his eyes darting around as if the traitor is somewhere in the room.

"That's not for you to worry about. Get dressed. You're coming with us."

Sitting up from the table, he holds the small towel around him. "Like hell I am," he scoffs.

"You have one minute to put some fucking clothes on."

He's looking worse for wear. He's gotten pudgy and soft in the middle, his hairline is receding, his skin is pale, and the wrinkles around his eyes and mouth are a testament to his time spent in hiding without care.

He looks like shit.

"You know," he says, reaching for his clothes on the table next to him, "I thought you'd have come a long time ago for me."

"I needed time to dismantle everything you built. I'm a patient man. My father taught me that."

Joey laughs bitterly. "I'm sure he did."

My jaw pops as I clench it closed. He's going to find out just how much my father taught me soon enough.

"You need to hurry. There's movement on the south east side of the property. I don't have a visual on who it is," Stefano says to us.

"Clear a path back for us," I order. "Let's fucking go." I nod at Dante, and once Joey has his pants and shirt on, he binds his hands behind his back with zip ties.

With his paranoia, Dom and Geno told us their father wanted to have this entire section of the house to himself so he knew no one was listening in or watching him, which plays right into our hands. There's no one around to see, hear, or stop us from taking the bastard.

I'm in the middle of the pack behind Dante and Joey, when a voice comes through our intercoms.

"Men coming through back door!" Then we hear shots ring out from below us.

"Fuck! Stef, we need another way!" I yell.

"They're down! Keep coming!"

I push at Joey's back and we stay the course.

"You won't make it off the property with me," he taunts, laughing.

"Shut the fuck up," I growl.

We make it back down the large, curved staircase, and I turn to see four bodies lying dead with pools of blood around them.

"You mother fuckers!" he bellows just as more men flood in from the back of the house.

I shove Joey behind me and grab my gun from my left shoulder holster, ducking down behind the banister. I fire off shots in two quick successions each, hitting the men center mass as they round the corner to where we are.

The entryway has a matching staircase on the other side that leads up to a balcony on the second-floor, and Alec runs across to assume the same position as me behind the other banister. He takes care of the men who are coming from around the other side with the same practiced ease as me.

"We've got it, Boss!" one of my men, Anthony, yells when there's a pause in action. "Get to the car!"

Dante hoists Joey off the floor and pushes him out the door. I nod to Alec and we follow them out the door and into the waiting SUV. "Where the fuck is Luca?!"

"He was behind us upstairs. I lost him after that," Alec says.

"Fuck! Find Luca!" I yell to everyone on the coms. "He was last seen upstairs!"

"On it!" Then a few second go by. "Got him! He's on his way down!"

I'm seething. Luca knows not to pull bullshit like this. I'm not losing anyone else to this fucking family.

I see him bounding out the front door, and *what the fuck?* He has a girl by the arm, pulling her along with him.

Opening the trunk door, Luca lifts her up and sets her in the back.

"Alfie, go," I growl angrily when Luca gets in beside me. I don't have time to ask if he's lost his damn mind. We have to get out of here.

"All men are out and accounted for," I hear from Stefano when we make it out of the gates, and I take my intercom out of my ear and dial Gabriel's number.

"Make the exchange," I clip, then hang up without hearing his response.

The soft cries of the girl in the back fill the quiet space and I turn to Luca. "There better be a good fucking reason for this."

"Later," is all he says, and I turn to look at Alec in the seat behind us who gives me a slight shake of his head, telling me he doesn't know what the fuck Luca is thinking either.

I drop it for now, not wanting to scare the poor girl further. We don't hurt innocent women, so I know there has to be a reason Luca would take Angela Cicariello, Joey's daughter, and Dom and Geno's sister.

On first glance, I'd say she's around eighteen to twenty years old, but I'm going to have a serious problem with my brother if he's doing anything other than rescuing her from her fucked up family.

I can hear her teeth clattering, and glance back to meet her wide, scared eyes. She's curled into the corner of the trunk with her arms wrapped around her legs, shaking. I mean, Jesus, she's dressed in nothing more than a pair of shorts and a tank top.

Luca looks back as well, and then sighs. Taking his coat off, he hands it back to her, but she doesn't move, so he tosses it at her. Angela looks at him with such disdain that I wonder again what the fuck he was thinking taking her.

Now's not the time to ask, though. Especially in front of her.

The drive back to Manhattan feels twice as long as the ride out to Long Island, but when we eventually get back, the adrenalin I had pumping through my veins during the firefight comes back when I see Dante dragging Joey from the trunk and through the garage.

Angela lets out a surprised gasp when she sees her father. "Oh my God," she whispers, so low I barely hear her.

"I've got her," Luca says. "Then I'll meet you down there."

I pin him with a stare that has him swallowing hard. "You have a lot to explain." Climbing out of the vehicle, I head to the elevator with Alec, Vinny, and Nico, and we ride the next car down.

Dante has Joey on his knees in the middle of the mats in the gym.

Let the fun begin.

CHAPTER 34
Abrianna

"How was your lunch with Shelby?" Leo asks me when I walk through the door. He's sitting on the couch with a folder of papers, his arm slung casually over the back of the couch, and the sleeves of his white dress shirt rolled up with the top two buttons undone at his throat.

My God, he's sexy.

The fact that I get to come home to this is beyond my wildest dreams. There was a time I thought I would have to learn to be okay with being alone for the rest of my life.

I sigh, rubbing my forehead. "As good as could be expected." After talking everything out with Leo, I decided it was best to dissolve my branch of the foundation and donate whatever money and supplies we had amongst all of the places we supported. That was the only way I was going to be guaranteed that it would never be used to smuggle anything ever again.

I didn't want to do it anymore. It didn't feel right. I don't know if it's more because of my father and Sam, or because it's where I used to spend all of my time trying to forget Leo. Probably both.

I still love helping people, but I can't let it be my life anymore. I was working on a scale too big to control everything. I missed helping people, hands on.

I just came from telling Shelby that she was out of a job, and it was hard. She's been such a good friend to me, and I had to lie to her as to why the charity was dissolving.

She was upset, but I told her I was able to get her a job at another foundation I have connections with.

Even harder, was telling my mother. She didn't believe me at first. But then I took her to the apartment Leo set my father up in a few floors below his penthouse that's guarded 24/7, and he told her everything. She was as in the dark as I was, but for so much longer. And the fucked-up part was that she got over it in a minute.

They're not even going to close the foundation. I only had the power and leverage to insist on closing the New York branch, but they love their life too much to give up any aspect of it. They're taking Sam with them too.

Apparently my mother has fewer morals than I thought.

I walked out after that.

I'm so done being a Fleming. I'm ready to be a Carfano.

"Come here, angel." Leo points to the spot next to him, and I gladly take it. His arm immediately pulls me close and I lean my head against his shoulder. "I have a proposition for you," he says low, his voice velvety smooth.

"If you use that voice, you can proposition anything from me," I say without thought, and he tightens his arm around me.

Leaning in close, he whispers, "Don't temp me right now, angel. I'm trying to be good."

"Try a little less."

Groaning, Leo turns my head and gives me a hard kiss that's over way too quickly.

"I want you to have everything," he rasps against my lips. "I know it hurt you to let it all go, but if you want to start over, you can."

"What?" I pull back to look into his eyes. "What do you mean?"

"I mean, you can do whatever you want. If you want to start your own charity, you can. What's mine is yours, angel. Or you can just volunteer. I remember you telling me after we first met that you love working with people and seeing your impact firsthand."

"You remember that?"

"I remember everything you've ever told me."

Smiling, I pull him in for a kiss that has my entire body lighting up in flames. "Thank you," I murmur between kisses.

"Anything for you."

Pulling away, I stand and hold my hand out to him. "No, anything for you," I say with a smile, and he flashes me his wolfish predatory grin. I'll happily be his prey for the rest of my life, letting him catch me, devour me, and then breathe life back into me so he can chase me all over again.

Picking me up at the waist, Leo hauls me over his

shoulder and takes off through the house, tossing me down on the bed in our room.

"If it's anything I want, I have a few ideas, angel."

"So do I." I smirk, and he growls, pulling me by my ankles back to him. His dark eyes are telling me everything I need to know. He loves me, but he fully intends on giving me his darkness right now.

And I wouldn't have it any other way.

ACKNOWLEDGMENTS

Thank you to everyone who took a chance on Casino King and my mafia world! I know it was a drastic change from my little coastal town in Maine, but mafia runs through my veins (not for real, I wish!). And THANK YOU to everyone who has had kind words to say about it!

ABOUT THE AUTHOR

Rebecca is a dreamer through and through with permanent wanderlust. She has an endless list of places to go and see, hoping to one day experience the world and all it has to offer.

She's a Jersey girl who dreams of living in a place with freezing cold winters and lots of snow! When she's not writing, you can find her planning her next road trip and drinking copious amounts of coffee (preferably iced!).

Website, blog, shop, and links to all social media:
www.rebeccagannon.com

Follow me on Instagram to stay up-to-date on new releases, sales, teasers, giveaways, and so much more!
@rebeccagannon_author

Printed in Great Britain
by Amazon